# LYNNE RUSSELL

## PJ Santini Series Book 3

# Love Heels!

## The TV news business can be murder

NIGHTTRAINBOOKS

# Praise for Lynne Russell and The PJ Santini Series

"CNN's Lynne Russell is back, in an explosion of page-turning talent. Get your best bottle of wine, your favorite couch, and prepare for one wild night with *Hell On Heels*. It's a helluva read!"

– Craig Nelson, New York Times best-selling author
of *Rocket Men* and *The First Heroes*

"PJ Santini...is the love child of Janet Evanovich and Elmore Leonard. Lynne Russell's spunky private eye had me at PJ's peeing into a one-pound coffee can during stakeouts. It is just so Jeff Bridges' burnt-out country singer in *Crazy Heart*, before the love of a good woman took all the piss out of him."

– Rita Zekas, *Toronto Star*

"Talk about a Renaissance woman, Lynne Russell does it all!"

– *Warner Bros. Television*

"Hilarious! PJ Santini's hardboiled detective banter is as sharp and sexy as her stilettos. A humor-mixed-with-murder mystery romp featuring a roster of brash, street-smart characters, in this fast-paced riff on hard-boiled detective fiction."

– Rhonda Rovan, Beauty Editor, *Best Health/Readers Digest*

"Step aside Jack Reacher, PJ Santini is the new bad ass on the scene, actually a very fine ass to be precise. In *Hell On Heels*, her debut caper, she busts chops and cops, while tricked out in her push-up bras, thigh highs and skimpy bikini panties...when she's not going commando. Nobody's playmate, but easily a future Miss November, we can't wait for her next titillating adventure."

– Jeff Cohen, Exec Editor/Publisher *Playboy* Special Editions, Playboy Enterprises

"*Hell On Heels* should come with a warning label! Lynne Russell's masterful depiction of female investigator PJ Santini can literally raise your pulse rate to dangerous levels. The brilliantly crafted insights a reader gets into the thought processes of the clever, gutsy, tough-talking yet sexually vulnerable Santini is alone worth the price of admission."

– Ted Kavanau, Founder of *CNN Headline News*

"PJ Santini is actually Lynne Russell late at night with wine, lights out, imagination gone wild. Both of them are Columbo without the cigar and appendage. Oh the joy of thinking you've been invited to ride shotgun and look for her weapons stash."

– *Moby-In-The-Morning*, Moby Enterprises

"A news anchor with the personality of a professional wrestler."

– *The New York Times*

## About the Author

LYNNE RUSSELL anchored CNN for 18 years, the first woman to anchor a regular network nightly newscast, over 33,000 of them. For her unbiased dedication to the People's Right to Know, The New York Times called her a "just-the-facts stalwart of CNN Headline News". They also called her a news anchor with the personality of a professional wrestler, which she took as a compliment. In the Washington Journalism Review: a spot as *Best in the Business*. A private investigator, double black belt, and former Deputy Sheriff, Lynne now writes romantic crime novels. She and her husband live near Washington, D.C. and in Italy.

## About PJ Santini

PJ SANTINI lives in an uncharted corner of Lynne's brain. When PJ spends long, boring hours stuck in a car on a surveillance job, she amuses herself by counting all the places on her body where she can stash her gun – she's up to twelve, now – and she wishes to thank Lynne for the idea. It helps to make up for the indignity of having to pee into a one-pound coffee can.

## About this Book

NO GOOD DEED goes unpunished. It puts you in the crosshairs. Of a murder rap, or a Meaningful Domestic Relationship. Which is more dangerous? PJ Santini, private investigator and television news reporter, is dusting off her Louboutin stilettos after a 2 a.m. cemetery shootout in Buffalo, NY. Already, her tanned, toned PI boss's new society divorce case is turning into a homicide investigation.

It may kill her, but it won't get in the way of Chianti and pasta. Ma cooks. Pop works Cold Cases in the basement between meals. PJ wants those leggings that compress fat, pushing blood up to your temples and swelling your lips to new fullness with a perky smile that looks like you're passing gas. Her Sicilian Nonna, whose specialty is revenge, is jilted by her lover and invents *Bidet* therapy. Her "connected" cousin, Sandro "The Eel" DiLeo, needs a favor. What could go wrong?

# ALSO BY LYNNE RUSSELL

FICTION:
*Hell On Heels* (NightTrainBooks)
*Heels Of Fortune* (NightTrainBooks)

NONFICTION:
*How To Win Friends, Kick Ass and Influence People*
(St Martin's Press)

FIRST EDITION, SEPTEMBER 2020

Published by NightTrainBooks.

Cover design by DesignzbyDanielle

Book design by Maureen Cutajar
www.gopublished.com

Library of Congress Cataloging-in-Publication Data applied for.

ISBN print edition: 978-1-7327610-5-6
ISBN e-book edition: 978-1-7327610-4-9

*With gratitude and love to my husband, Chuck de Caro,*
*for his relentless faith in me and his fearless editing...*
*or is it his relentless editing and his fearless faith in me.*

*For Renate*

PJ Santini Series Book 3

# Love Heels!

## The TV news business can be murder

# CHAPTER ONE

## The morning after

S o how was your night?" I asked him, gulping Colombian roast from a diner mug with somebody else's lipstick on it.

On general principles, I try to start off the day not remembering what I did the night before, even if it was my fault. Men do this, and they wind up carrying a lot less baggage into the morning. For men, every day is a new adventure. Nothing we think we taught them in the previous twenty-four hours makes it through the night.

But I knew exactly how Daly's night had gone. We'd been caught up in the moment, mixing business with pleasure, and things had gotten so far out of hand, I was going to have to retire the number on my favorite French lace red teddy. I was trying hard not to think of it as love. But who wouldn't fall for him?

By breakfast we – my private detective boss, Tango Daly, and I – had put ourselves back together and had gone on to wrap up the paperwork on the 2 a.m. graveyard shootout. We hadn't hung around Buffalo's oldest and finest cemetery to talk to the cops, and they still hadn't come for our version. Why not? The coffee was cooling off fast under the paddle fans, and the guy in the next booth was having trouble lighting another cigarette in the breeze.

This worried me, because only a cop would chain smoke in a place like this, with *No Smoking* signs everywhere, and not even order toast.

He also was making notes while we talked. Daly caught it, too. Somebody obviously thought, maybe hoped, that there'd be more to our story than we'd write into our official report, and they could charge us with obstructing justice. They'd have to go through every detail, and it would take some time for them to fabricate the rest, but the danger was there. It was always there.

"What should we do?" I asked him, rolling my eyes toward the cop.

"You're exhausted," he said, his voice soft and his quick smile aimed right at me. I wondered if this was just for effect, or something more. That would be new for a big, tough guy. He patted the table and swept his hand to the right to signal *Be patient, be quiet.* "We've done everything right. I'm waiting to hear from the police, so we can cooperate fully and give them all the information they need." He said it slowly, so the goon with the pen could get it all.

When the adrenaline had worn off this morning, and all the *Discharge of a Firearm on a Case* forms had been filled out and filed, we left Daly's Iroquois Investigations office on Elmwood Avenue in his fancy black BMW stealthmobile, to do a post-mortem here in our "other office", *First Watch.*

*First Watch* is a place where you can get eggs, bacon and home fries all day and all night. Situated enough blocks away from Iroquois to be convenient, but still not on the radar. It has lots of windows for a good view of the parking lot, and a mirror on the back wall, if you have the bad luck to sit facing the wrong direction.

This particular mirror had an extra asset: an emergency exit conveniently located right next to it. Back in the day, this entire chain of diners was built the same way. Very popular with private investigators who have to meet with unstable clients and sources, people who are one group therapy session from making the front page. You don't want them coming to your office.

We'd been playing with our food for fifteen minutes, giving the Precinct every opportunity to approach us if they wanted to, when my cell phone blasted its new ringtone: *Magnum PI*. The old one was *Mission Impossible*, the story of my life. Magnum was more carefree, but he got the job done and was cut some slack for his mistakes. I figured change your ringtone, change your luck.

"It's Benny." Benny Levin, the crime reporter from *The Buffalo News*. In New York State, people actually still read the paper. I like to think it's because they see the value of holding the written word in their hand. My father, a retired police officer who runs a Cold Case operation out of his basement, has a different theory.

"If you try hard enough, you can still get high off of newsprint," Pop says. "You do the math."

The phone's vibrating dance across the scarred formica table was mesmerizing.

"I'm not answering it."

"Answer it," Daly said, glancing over at the cop, who looked to be about thirteen years old and on his first surveillance job. He was tall and beefy, but Mom probably wouldn't let him go out for football. His head was cocked toward us like an Irish setter waiting for a treat.

We were pretty certain nobody knew the whole story. And why should they? We'd done nothing wrong, unless it's a crime to narrowly escape death at the hands of two homicidal maniacs who happen to be in the same place – a graveyard, for god's sake – at the same time. And they weren't even working together.

Information about that would definitely be on a need-to-know basis. My job was to give the newspaper enough to stay friends, but not give the eavesdropper anything that would fill in the blanks for the man perpetually out to destroy me, Chief Homicide Detective Frank Longoria. I asked Benny why in the world he was calling me, of all people. With 900-thousand residents in Erie County, New York, and 250-thousand of them hunkered down right here in town, he calls me?

"I got you on a tip," he said.

"From?"

"From a reliable source."

"And who would that be? Or is it a secret?"

"No, no. No secret at all. In fact, he said you'd ask, and he said I should be sure to tell you exactly. It was Detective Frank Longoria. He said to tell you he's head of the BPD Homi..."

"I know where he works!" I hissed. *Easy PJ, don't let it show. Junior Crimefighter, over there, will write it down and Frank will know he got to you.* I told him to hang on, and put down the phone.

4

"Yo! Could we have a warm-up here? And no cream, don't dilute it."

Yolanda Gomez is the most intuitive waitress ever. We've had lots of discussions about how coffee – and certain other things in life – are strictly to be enjoyed, and how extras like cream are really essentials. So she picked up on that, the no cream, and on the building tension, and the need to buy time. She poured the boiling hot coffee very slowly. One deep whiff of its pungent, just-brewed aroma sent little men with jack-hammers up into my sinuses, kick-starting my pre-frontal cortex into creative thinking. The coffee was so strong, pulses of seismic explosions blew across brain synapses that had thought they'd never see action again. When the idea finally came, I turned the tables on Benny. I decided to manufacture a false lead that would send them all away.

"I probably shouldn't tell you this, Benny," stage-whispering through another mouthful of coffee, "but if you hear there's an out-of-country connection, that's out-of-country, it's true. It's very hush-hush. I'll say no more."

"So then, what I've heard is right. I promise not to tell a soul," Benny said as he pulled up the number for his contact in Racketeering Division.

# CHAPTER TWO

## *Journey*

W ell, there it was. Longoria still wanted me gone. I'd known him all my life, and he'd always been the one who didn't play by the rules. Juvenile Delinquent Makes Good. Worse than that, he was in tight with the Mob. Very tight. And he knew I knew. I could probably prove it if I had to. *Probably,* if I didn't mind jeopardizing my entire family, including the ones who also engaged in Frank's questionable sideline, like my connected cousin Sandro "The Eel" DiLeo, of the Belleville, New Jersey DiLeos.

Ma thought Sandro was adorable; my best friend Vicky thought he was hot and was engaged to marry him; I couldn't help liking him for the fuss he made over me, and the times he'd helped out when I was working a case. Like interpreting threatening notes written in Mobspeak. Pop saw the rest of the story, in a penal kind of way. Family gatherings worked out as long as the food and the wine lasted.

Daly dropped me off back at Iroquois. Sitting at the curb out front, in my beloved silver Mercedes SLK, Sweet Boy, it was still early in the day. I wondered what new hell was in store. They'd be waiting for me at the television station where I was more or less steadily employed as an investigative reporter. If I showed up now, the news director would be leaning in my office in two seconds, sending me out on a job nobody else would take. It didn't matter how adept I was at developing great crime stories, to him I was just Lois Lane. Granted, the crime stories wound up involving me, but that's not the point.

I was about to act like an adult and go on over anyway, when a call came in from *Chickie's Pawn Shop*.

Chickie Vecchio was an old buddy of Pop's on the Organized Crime Task Force. He'd come across "a thing that maybe hangs on a necklace, what do you call 'em, a thing, an amulet. It just came in. A guy I know, he's got a pawn shop in Belleville, in New Jersey. Once a month he's here, I don't ask why. Just for the hell of it we trade a box of stuff that didn't sell. This thing's interesting but not worth much, kinda old and broke.

"Speaking of which," he said, "why don't you come around an' say hi to your ole Uncle Chickie, and have a look at the same time."

I really needed something in my day that didn't come with complications, so I jumped at the chance.

"You got it! Be there in ten!" But I was still wearing clothes messed up from crawling around in the cemetery. Not my best look. With no time to change, I threw the gearshift into Park and popped open the back, the Trunk of Miracles. It's filled with useful investigative toys including blonde and brunette wigs, makeup case, hardhat, clipboard, dark blue windbreaker that says OFFICIAL on the back in subtle block letters, eyeglasses with no correction, and bowling shoes I found at Goodwill. And Oreos. Also, by chance, a bitchin' pair of Christian Louboutin black leather stiletto ankle boots – smooth as butter – that I'd spent a fortune on, but hardly ever wore because they were made for just one thing, and it wasn't walking.

On the other hand, shoes like that could change your day. That, and the attitude you'd need to show up in them when the rest of your clothes looked like you'd just come from a casting call for an undead movie.

I took Wilming over to Chester, then deliberately overshot the target and did a U-turn, winding up a good distance from the shop, and from whoever might be on his way in with last night's take. Chickie's Pawn is on every professional thief's speed dial. Not that Chickie knowingly accepts stolen property; in fact, he makes so many calls to Robbery Division at the Precinct, they should put in a hotline. But face it, there's a better than average chance the goods are so new they still have barcodes and the original owners' breath on them.

Chickie was waiting with a big bear hug, over by the jewelry display case. It struck me that he and Pop had worked together so long, they'd begun to look alike. Round face, thinning grey hair, twinkling Italian eyes, and both with a penchant for khaki slacks and paper thin, thousand-year-old white T-shirts. Also, because of their line of work, both were uncommonly aware of life's twists and turns, and of the passage of time.

I had a look at it, that broken amulet. It was more like a weathered coin, weighty enough to roll around in your hand, with a sort of squiggly design. It felt pleasing, but oddly un-comfortable. Impatient for the moment to be over.

"My grandmother... you know Nonna Giovanna, she's here from Sicily... she says everything comes with its own vibrations," I told him. "And damn, this definitely has something to say."

"Tell you what. It'll never sell. It's gold, but only good for scrap. Take it, I give it to you." He was a sweetheart. "It came in with a bunch of other stuff. I think it has some history, y'know, goes back in time. Maybe you'll figure it out. Or give it to your grandma. I hear she could use something to take her mind off the Harley dude."

"You know about that?" I couldn't believe there was so little going on in Buffalo that Nonna's love interest would make the headlines.

"Never a dull moment at the house, eh? Your Pop told me. He was real worried about his mother. What could a super-sized aging Hells Angel see in a pint-size ancient Sicilian broad? No offense."

"None taken. In a way, the appeal is easy: Nonna embraces life with complete abandon. She's exactly the female you want on your Hog, hangin' back in the sissy seat, screaming into the wind as you rip off a liquor store and peel out at 60 mph."

"Yeah, but again with all due respect, she don't know she's left the Old Country. When the bitchin' broad riding behind you is all in black, showing off boots and fringe, it's supposed to be motorcycle boots and leather fringe. Not black high-top Oxfords and a Palermo shawl. *Capice?*"

"Well, it's all over now," I told him. "He dumped her for a forty-year-old hair stylist with a special talent for, you should pardon the expression, blow drying."

"*Ho capito.*" Chickie understood perfectly. "When I first became a cop, they told me that whenever you look for a motive for somethin', you should always start with money. Since then, I've revised it. Never underestimate the power of the BJ." He winked. "Now, don't go telling your Pop I talk about that with you. He thinks you're still nine."

"Thanks, Uncle Chickie. I'm going to go change clothes before I face the family." I gave him a kiss on the cheek, and heard him call out as the bell jangled on the front door.

"Tell your Pop I've got a lead on a cold case that's about to turn very hot!"

My condo is downtown, six floors up in a ten-story building right on Lake Erie, luxurious by my standards. The road from there to the part of town known as Lovejoy has been traveled in happiness and sadness; but always in the knowledge that it was home, the place I grew up. The few square blocks where my family has lived since Dominic and Margie Santini fell in love at a St. Agatha of Catania church supper, got married, set up shop, and brought my brother and me into this world. Italians from the Old Country dubbed it Iron Island, because it's in the middle of a nest of railroad tracks. Not the most glamorous part of Buffalo, but a testament to family values, love of country, and personal responsibility. And an appreciation of what those things can bring to you, and to the people you touch in your life.

*IF* you can stay out of jail. That's frequently an issue. If you can't, you might be running into former schoolmate Frank Longoria, ironically no stranger to jail time himself. Or you could meet my brother Tony, a cable guy with ADHD and big plans to open a Sicilian seafood restaurant called The Garlic Cove. Or my best friend Vicky, who's studying up to be a Mafia princess, whether she admits it or not. I don't think she realizes how high her hair is getting. If Sandro gives her any more gold necklaces, something spinal is going to pop. Vicky runs *Balducci's Love Your Dog*, where canines can get pedicures and star treatment for a day or a month.

So with the car tucked into the safety of the garage under my building, I swiped the ElectroPass and took the elevator up to the apartment that my designer shoes allowed me to share with them. Locking the door behind me, I yearned to sleep until tomorrow... wearing something soft and amorphous, who's gonna see it... sitting up in bed first with comfort food, maybe mashed potatoes.

But duty called, so I pulled Lovejoy clothes out of the closet. A nice, fitted white Brooks Brothers no-iron shirt, and black jeans with a lot of stretch. Before I'd finished backing up for a look, the full-length mirror was screaming *Catholic school! You're back in Catholic school!* So I untucked the shirt and unbuttoned it down to where my mother would have a fit. Then it was obvious that the best shoes would be the ones I'd just taken off, the Louboutin red-soled ankle boots with the impossible heels.

# CHAPTER THREE

## No good deed goes unpunished

Chickie must have talked with Pop, because the whole family was waiting on the front lawn when I pulled up. It was so Norman Rockwell, it took my breath away. Relatives who actually liked each other, standing in front of a working class house that wasn't fancy, but you could tell the effort had been made. Difference is, Rockwell's people aren't all talking at once. And eating.

It's a known fact that Italians convert food directly into noise. Lunchtime was closing in, and everybody was prepping. Tony was throwing down a big, sloppy meatball sandwich. Pop and Ma were doing stovetop quality control, polishing off big chunks of crusty homemade bread dipped in bubbling red sauce. Nonna, who never seems to gain weight, was munching on a piece of Parmesan cheese. Seriously, if she were a kitchen utensil she'd be one of those Brillo pads with a skinny black handle on a big cartoon shoe stand, her short hair bearing a striking resemblance to the curly steel Brillo mesh. Her thick ebony stockings, dress, and clunky shoes are the icing on the *cannoli*.

We all headed across the lawn toward the house, my heels aerating the grass as they sank into it. Instinctively we went single file, knowing that when we got to the living room picture window we'd be hanging a sharp right to parade up the narrow front steps.

"So," Tony said as soon as the screen door closed, "who did the shootin'? Word is, it was all your fault."

"Who told you that?" I snapped back, looking for something to wipe my shoes with, knowing the answer.

"Just the grapevine. Forget about it. It doesn't mean anything. Sorry I said it, it didn't come out right."

"It's okay. I know it started with Longoria." All anybody had to do was to drop a few words to Antje Pooler, the main cashier at Eccola's grocery store, and it was all over town inside of twenty minutes. Everybody in the neighborhood passed through that store, and they had mothers with telephones, husbands in bowling leagues, daughters with nail appointments, and sons who shot the breeze during oil changes and house arrest. Frank would know this, know that the rumor would get back to me.

"Here, taste this," Ma said, shoving a wooden spoon in my mouth. It was sweet ricotta with little bits of citron, for dessert. Heaven. I got a soup spoon for more, and she hit me with, "A minute in the mouth, a lifetime on the hips."

"Thanks a lot. If you're going to say this every time, why do you ask me to eat?" See, this is why I wear stretch pants. It's also why I wear the classiest heels I can afford. My theory is, you can't control everything but you can sure control the way you present it. Even to yourself.

There was only one place to unveil Chickie's gift: the dining room table, the scene of all Italian family business when it's not in the kitchen, where there's a counter with carving knives lined up.

"Chickie, he's so sweet, he gave me this pretty little jewelry thing. I haven't cleaned it up yet. He knows gold when he sees it, but he says there's no value beyond that." I pushed it to the center of the table, so everybody could have a look. Nonna dug into the pocket of her always-ready-for-a-funeral black dress and found her reading glasses. They were at the bottom, under Keenex and the pouch of herbs she carried for banishing negative energy in emergencies. For Nonna, fighting evil is a full-time job.

"Nobody got robbed for this, I'll tell you that." Pop finally decided, waving it off and leaning back into his chair.

Tony, ever the optimist, turned it over like he was showing a card at poker. "It's pretty in its own way."

"Turn it back," Ma said,."There's something about it. You can't take your eyes off it. It looks like... almost like..."

"Like nothing! *Niente! Don't touch it!*" Nonna was breathing with an effort, struggling with the knot on the herbs. "This is bad! This is very bad! Just when I thought I was out, they pull me back in!"

"*Godfather?*" I mumbled at Pop.

"No, still the Sopranos. She was watching when I got up."

My grandmother, Pop's mother, never took English classes. Her dialogue is basically whatever she picks up in the house, jacked up with lines from movies and television. Not foolproof, but effective. It was beginning to worry us that we knew exactly what she meant.

"What're you talking? You've only been here in Buffalo a few weeks," Ma said, getting up to serve the pasta and effectively ending the discussion. "You couldn't possibly have even seen it before. I hope."

With that, Nonna exploded. "I see nothing!" Nonna cried, staring down the bauble and furiously waving a sprig of dried rosemary at it as she backed away. "I know nnnnnothing!"

"Hogan's Heroes!" we shouted in unison.

I set the table for the five of us while Pop filled me in on some of the cases he was working in the corner of the basement. The Ice Pack, they called themselves, retired law enforcement on a mission, and on a budget. The only extra they could afford was their own phone line.

We'd just settled into the living room to stay out of Ma's way and let the meal proceed, when a terrible racket started in the second floor hallway. At first, all we could hear was Nonna. This was not unreasonable, given her years of practice. Even in Palermo, when the fairer sex elicits quicker attention from a male by upping the decibels, it gets to be a habit.

"You say you try...you try. Well, do or do not. Isa no try! Ama tell you, now is not a good time for recipes!"

The discriminatory mechanism Nonna's brain used to pull quotes out of films and then pop them into conversation remains a mystery. This time it was *Star Wars*. Yoda is confusing enough without an Italian accent.

Tony's bedroom was next to Nonna Giovanna's room, which had been mine. The family still called it PJ's room. I didn't move out of the house until I got serious with a guy from college. I got married – and then widowed. All in the same week, I might add. Tony has moved out to live with girlfriends who made him miserable so many times we call his room Rehab. He was standing in her doorway.

"All I said, Nonna, was I'm trying to understand why you won't give me some more recipes for my restaurant. See, here, they're all in this notebook. We're almost ready! Pop said he'd front me some money if I saved $5,000, and I've almost got it."

Tony and his calorie-challenged, blimp-like friend Carmine both worked for the cable company. They'd been making plans for their restaurant through years of boring modem hookups and irate customers.

"And Carmine's got some money, too."

"You no afraid he'll eat all the profits?" Nonna slow-pitched.

"I keep telling you, it's glandular!"

"No itsa not! It's *fettuccini Alfredo!*"

"Does this have something to do with that jewelry thing?"

"Never you mind," she warned. "Itsa no good. There's a bad omen today, very bad. Nobody moves, nobody gets hurt."

"But..." Tony could see his dreams fading. Without her recipes he had nothing.

"Enough! Ama gonna chill out, you understand?" Nonna's door slammed and she stormed down the hall. "Ama gonna sit on the *bidet.*"

"On the what?!" I shouted upstairs.

"On the *bidet!*"

"But we don't have a *bidet,*" I said mostly to myself.

"Oh, yes we do," Pop said. "Carmine's been working extra as a plumber's helper to save money for the restaurant. Gotta hand it to him, working two jobs."

I was confused. "So he used his money to buy Nonna a bum washer?"

"Not exactly." Pop glanced around to calculate his chances of finishing a story, himself. In this house, delivering a punchline is a competitive sport. "Carmine installed it. Heated seat that replaces the regular one. Just press a button. Very fancy jets of warm water hit the high spots. Sandro brought it over. Apparently it had fallen off of a truck and he just happened to find it in the road." Which was Pop's way of saying the boy from Belleville was still connected, and Pop's own mother's fanny was caught up in fraudulent fancy.

"And she sits on it because...?"

"Leave her alone. It's her drug of choice. Could be worse. Has been worse."

My father and I sat in the living room in silence to contemplate the mysteries of life, trying to shake the image of my grandmother getting her kicks on the thunderbox. In the kitchen, Ma was banging around in a refrigerator drawer, probably for more Parmesan, Nonna having polished off the hunk that had been set aside for the pasta. I would have gone in to help, but Pop discourages any alteration of the battle plan during Ma's final phase of cooking. Since he retired, mealtimes had become even more important, and nothing should get in the way.

"If it weren't for cold cases, I'd go nuts around here," Pop said, reading my mind.

"You know, Uncle Chickie was only trying to do a nice thing. He thought we'd enjoy the mystery of it. He should never know all the trouble it caused. Oh, by the way, I guess he told you he has an important lead on a cold case."

"Yep." That was about all the information I'd get about it. There were things he couldn't discuss with me, because they were ongoing police business. There were things I couldn't discuss with him, either because they involved PI case privacy or because they would've made him worry about me even more than he already did.

"Let's eat! *Cannoli* for dessert!" Ma marched to the table proudly bearing a platter of pasta, with meatballs browned to perfection. Tony galloped to the kitchen to retrieve the pot of steaming red sauce, and I went in for the salad and the hot bread. I could feel my thighs beginning to expand.

Nonna appeared, looking calm and refreshed. We all struggled not to notice.

# CHAPTER FOUR

## *It creeps up on you*

Ma whipped off her apron, signaling it was time for everybody to sit. No sooner had we done that, than my cell phone rang in my purse. I ignored it. At the Santinis, food takes precedence over everything. Then the house phone rang. It stopped.

"Nobody move," Ma said deliberately. Her gaze landed on the black touch tone wall model, probably the last one in existence, daring it to make a sound.

It rang again. And did not stop.

Nonna's Oxfords covered the distance in one leap. "*Pronto!*" Then, "It's for you," dragging me by a bicep pinch away from the table.

"I don't know who this is," I said loud enough for Ma to hear, "but we're just sitting down to lunch, so it had better be good."

"It is," Johnny Renza said. "I need you to get over here fast. There's a great story breaking, and I thought Soper would give it to you when I told him about it, but he's going to assign it to the new guy. You need to be here now!"

"Is it just that you're upset the new newsroom stud is going to get a break?" Renza would always be rested, ready and hot, but why inflate an ego that was about to burst, anyway.

"Be serious, Janice. I know that over the years I haven't been exactly fair to you, or paid you the attention you deserve. I'm trying to make up for it. You've given me great stories, and I want to pay it forward."

"You're late."

"It's a term. Seriously, this is investigative."

"Then why don't you do it?"

"Got something else going."

Yeah, I bet. What's her name. I thought about that. And I thought about the pasta. I thought about the way he'd been a lowlife ever since high school, faithful in his own way but not in mine. I thought about pasta in general, and how the time I put into eating it is never wasted, unlike the time I put into expecting Renza to be sincere and then running out to an all-night pharmacy for a pregnancy test when I should have known all along he just can't help it.

Everybody was watching me suck my thumbnail, trying to decide what to do. I could use a good story.

"It's Johnny Renza," Tony said. "The thumb again."

"Okay," I told him. "Meet you in the newsroom?"

"Fast."

⌒‿

Sweet Boy barreled out of Lovejoy, and we caught Broadway to Sharpton, then over to Skyler Rd.

Must've been a helluva news day. The lot was so full, I had to create a parking spot next to the dumpster. The SLK, sleek, spotless and ready to be adored, didn't like that. I told him I'd make up for it after by taking him cruising in the valet parking drive of Masters Grand.

Masters Grand is the most exclusive and revered private club in Erie county. Revered by people with money and status, both of which can appear from out of nowhere, and vanish into thin air with the slightest hint of scandal or a bad quarterly earnings report. They vote you in and they vote you out.

Besides the perpetual cocktail hour in the leather-bound, brass nail-studded *Gentlemen's Towne Club* and in the mostly pink, tufted *Ladies' Private Affair,* it's all about golf; but also tennis and massages and fitness classes.

I always put Sweet Boy's top down first and then pull up slowly, as hopeful attendants jog out to meet us with visions of monster tips dancing in their heads. I do what I can to give the impression my curly red hair looks like cotton candy because of convertible wind. I'm positively alluring as we chitchat and get to know each other; then "a text comes in" and I have to leave right away.

Sweet Boy gets to be seen, the boys get a break in their day, and I'll have a better than average chance of getting inside for just a few minutes, some day when I really need it. It's just important to show up after shift change and on different days of the week, so they don't pick up on it or think I'm a hooker.

Renza was waiting for me at his desk, so I went straight to him and didn't even crack the door of my humble office. Murray Soper saw this and made a run for his own. I was there before he could lock the door. Knocking on the sign that said

NEWS DIRECTOR was strictly a courtesy, since I was going in anyway.

He pretended to be on the phone, some gibberish about lining up a photo shoot, and was out of breath from the quick dash. I took a chance.

"Forget it, Murray," I said louder, "I know all about it, and I want the story. I already have a lead on it. It's mine. Giving it to me is the only responsible thing to do."

"How could you possibly have a lead already?"

"It's what I do."

It was my impression that he knew less about it than I did, and was caught so completely off-guard that he had no comeback. I smiled, offered my hand, and he took it before he realized. Done.

Across the newsroom, Renza picked up the pace and followed me to my office. I'd inherited it from an investigative reporter who liked to be invisible, so it was away from the newsroom and close to the station's back door, for quick getaways. Like me, he'd been hardly ever there. Unfortunately when he *was* there, he was running an illegal operation that got him dead. I covered that. It almost got me dead, too.

While Renza and I were waiting for the fluorescents to come on, he took a seat in the visitor's chair and stretched his legs.

"Kinda reminds you of senior year, doesn't it? Lights out in the rec room till somebody's mom notices it and the fun is over." He was smiling in the dark.

"That was high school, Johnny." It made me smile, too.

"You had no complaints, as I recall," sending words across the room to me on a smooth wave of memory that caressed my face the way his fingers used to.

"That was before, well, before lots of things. It's like that old Statler Brothers song.... 'things get complicated when you get past eighteen'. But we did have a good time." It almost made me forget why we were here.

The fluorescents in the drop ceiling flickered to life, and we were back in the present.

"So now that Soper thinks I know so much about the story I even have a lead on it," I said, "maybe you'd better tell me what the hell it is."

Renza pushed the door closed.

"Open," I told him.

"We don't want other people to hear."

"Open."

"Which one of us don't you trust?" He gave me that look. The moony look that goes so well with his chestnut hair and Mediterranean tan and white linen suits, the look that always works with women.

When my breathing slowed, I told him, "Open it, please." And he did.

"So here's the thing," he said, settling back down. "A friend of mine goes to these sessions at a fitness club. I've been listening to her talk for a few weeks about one particular trainer. He works only with people who are already pretty well-developed, to help them sculpt their bodies. Not in a hardcore competitive way, more just putting a good finish on the product."

"He works with people? Which people?"

"Well, with women."

"Women. So, your friend is a woman. A pretty well-developed woman. Or maybe a pretty, comma, well-developed woman."

"Yes." You could tell Renza was feeling the slide into dangerous territory, and that didn't bother me at all. I loved it when he was uncomfortable.

"How well do you know this woman? Do I know this woman?" It'd better not be my nemesis, Kathy-the-bitch, who by chance also worked at the station.

"Know is such a tricky word. Let's just say she figures into this because I think there's a real story here."

"So what does she think is going on with this particular fitness trainer?"

"Well, he's becoming real friendly. Maybe too friendly. He's showing her pictures of himself wearing just that little sort of swimsuit bottom, all oiled up, posing like Mr. America or something." Renza was picking at his nails. He wanted very badly to bite off a little piece of cuticle.

"And you don't like that, do you?" My radar was up and going crazy. He was just jealous, and he wanted me to do something about it.

"C'mon, Renza. You don't like the attention she's getting, admit it. Fix it yourself!"

Summertime is hot enough without paying obligatory visits to gyms. To me, cardio involves simple kitchen equipment in the comfort of your own home. Open the refrigerator and remove a chilled 1.75 liter size *Jose Cuervo* pre-mixed *Golden Margarita with Grand Marnier* in the glass bottle. Take it by the neck and lift it ten times to the front, ten times to the side. Do the same thing with the other hand. Repeat until you get bored. Pour over ice and enjoy. (As days go by and the bottle empties, increase the number of reps to make up the difference.)

"But there's more." He got up and leaned into the doorframe, almost as if he wished he hadn't started it. "He's asking her if she'll pose for some pictures. Something creative."

That got my attention.

"I told her to go to another gym. But she won't do it, because it costs her practically nothing. Six months ago, there was a billing mixup and she hasn't paid a penny since."

"Well fine, she can do what she wants. I don't see how a place can stay in business that way. Their overhead's got to come from somewhere. What's this guy's name?"

"Lamar Jackson. His friends call him Lefty."

"Why?"

Renza looked surprised. "Could be because he's left-handed. But not entirely."

"So, then?" I wanted to know.

"Use your imagination, babe."

Oh god, not another one. "Renza, everywhere I go, everywhere I look, I'm surrounded by perverts! When I least expect it! Really, I can't do another one. I just can't. Not today."

Pregnant pause. "Your decision." He started to angle out the door. "But, just tell me one thing. Did you get into the news business and private investigation because you thought you wouldn't come across any perverts? Because if it weren't for perverts, neither of us would have anything to do. And you know it."

He was right. Which left me no excuse. All I could think was, *And I gave up pasta for this.*

# CHAPTER FIVE

## Walk this way

"Wait. Okay. Write down the name of the place and I'll go over tomorrow and have a look." I thanked Renza for the tip, stuffed the paper into my purse, and for half an hour tossed the puzzle around in my brain; after all, I was technically at work and should exert some effort. But it's been my experience that if you think for longer than thirty minutes, somebody will notice you don't look busy. Next thing you know, you really will be busy, and there goes the afternoon. So it wasn't hard to pack up and tiptoe out.

By the time I locked the door, I had no answers and felt completely deflated and not at all like playing the Masters Grand game. It wasn't like Renza to give me a big story. So if it was big, which I doubted, what did he have to gain from it?

More importantly, if I were going to scope out a place where guys were oiled up and babes were buffed up, what the hell was I going to put on my body? An invisibility cape would be good. I could keep my gun under there, too.

What I needed was those leggings with the high waist that they advertise on TV, the ones that trap everything where it's supposed to be and keep it there, and make it look half its size. From the look of the commercials, the compression of all that fat takes off ten years, apparently by pushing your blood supply to your temples, popping your eyes open to an innocent flirt, swelling your lips to new fullness, and painting your face with a wide perky smile that makes you look like you're passing gas. So I spent the rest of the day in Cheektowaga trolling Galleria Mall shops, looking for the impossible.

You never have a so-so experience in a gym. Never. You'll always come out of it with some lesson learned, something added to your life. Occasionally it has to be treated with antibiotics. Most of the time, it's the way you feel about yourself. You feel better for having pushed yourself, even if the push was only through the front door.

Or maybe it was an all-around shitty experience. Even then, you got something out of it. You just have to figure out what it was.

Sometimes you admire somebody's looks, and you wonder how long they've been at it. Or you wonder what the hell they're thinking in that outfit. If you really are ripped and sexy, your shirt doesn't have to say it.

You learn fashion sense. If you've got a few extra pounds on, then whatever you do, don't wear leggings with a predictable pattern like leopard or vertical stripes that will stretch out beyond recognition. And wear underwear. If your butt is tormenting the Spandex until it screams for mercy, people will take notice and vacate the area in case you blow. I saw that once, on a supremely hefty woman – Pop would call her "well fed". She looked like she'd hold, but when she lumbered into a squat, groaned and hoisted the barbell, fat burst out the back seam like yeasty pizza dough breaking free of plastic wrap in Ma's warm kitchen. Now, that's an image that won't die.

Or maybe you get lucky and find common ground with someone on a machine next to you. But that wasn't important now. I was going undercover tomorrow to find out what Lamar "Lefty" Jackson was all about.

It was a beautiful morning when, operating only on coffee and a wistful yearning for buttery croissants, I stepped out of the car on the expensive side of town. The place was called *Kettlebells*. This was in honor of those sissy-looking, ball-shaped weights with handles on them. Using them strengthens almost everything, as long as you don't let go. If you do, you can knock out somebody's teeth or take out a wall. Or, as in my case, bruise a cheek *and* break a toe when its concentrated ten pounds come into full-force contact with mere human flesh and bone.

I'd shoehorned myself into my old pink yoga outfit, which still looked pretty damn good... taking into account the occasional family-size double pack of Oreos during surveillance jobs, or when frustration eating just got the better of me. I'd seriously considered putting Sticky Notes all over my body, by way of explanation. Then if the folks inside Kettlebells were sympathetic and had a sense of humor, they'd know that I knew how it happened, and maybe they'd be gentle:

Stomach: *BAKED ZITI*
Right thigh: *ICE CREAM*
Left thigh: *GORGONZOLA*
Butt: *BREAD, BREAD, BREAD*
Right and left underarms: *CREAM* and *BUTTER*,
respectively.


I took one last look around the lot. No familiar cars, no faces that might question my presence.

Kettlebells stood by itself, a good hike from the road, surrounded by shrubbery, valet parking, and a few self-park slots so far back you did your cardio just walking to the building. Staff parked their cars in front, so that to passersby it would always look like business was good. Its double doors were protected by a fancy brown awning with white trim and crossed white kettlebells on the front. First thought: White chocolate bonbons on a bed of dark chocolate truffles. A person can skip breakfast, but she can't skip the memories.

Inside, it was pretty much like all the fitness clubs: groups of machines that worked different parts of the body; a bank of bicycles, and behind it an elevated bank of ellipticals. Printed workout motivation on the walls, like "No Limits" and "Sweat is My Body's Way of Saying Thanks!", and "You miss 100% of the shots you don't take". That last one seemed out of place, a famous Wayne Gretzky hockey quote.

"Who's the hockey fan?" I asked the $45 haircut standing inside the door. He was packed into a shiny brown Kettlebells shirt. No fabric wasted there, but on him it looked good.

"Dunno. You a member?" he asked, reaching across the counter for a clipboard.

"Nope, but I bet you have a free trial session, and I'd be interested in that."

"Yes, ma'am" he smiled big. "You are welcome to a Complimentary Training Experience." So we covered all the basics, he wanting everything but my blood type, and me supplying a fake name and as little information as possible, acting shy about it. I don't do shy very well. Dumb, yes. Shy, no. Some things just come more naturally.

After the quick tour, I told him I wanted to look around by myself. With every step, I sucked in my stomach more. Nobody laughed. It took some work to tighten my butt, strutting in five-year-old virtually virgin stiff running shoes. I remembered what the charm school lady had told me when I was fourteen. She said, "Keep your shoulders back and your chin up, and you will always look confident." It was working. Nobody was staring, so I guessed I fit in really well.

The Ab Cruncher was free, and I did a smooth slip onto the seat, like it was routine.

Who knew a breakthrough would happen so fast! I'd just raised my arms to grasp the two pull-down handles, which I admit did show off my bazookas to their maximum advantage, when from out of nowhere, another packed brown shirt with a name tag that said LAMAR showed up.

"Before you do that, pretty lady, let's talk about your back. I saw you walking. You've probably had a back injury recently. "

"A what?"

"Yeah, you looked pretty uncomfortable, like you were in pain," he said, closing in to keep it personal.

Uncomfortable? Humiliated would be more like it.

"New shoes, that's all," I shot back.

"Well, no problem." He eased off. "I haven't seen you here before. You new to Kettlebells?"

"Relatively. I haven't decided whether I want to sign up or not. I'll need a few more Complimentary Training Experiences, first."

"No problem. A girl as beautiful as you should have whatever she needs," he said to my chest. A real syrupy attitude for a guy who's known a woman for fifteen seconds. I put him about an inch taller than me, five-ten, 170 pounds of muscular real estate, ebony skin, disarming light brown eyes, blazing white teeth. His head was shaved and smoothed to the look of a shiny dark-roasted coffee bean, so as not to detract from the rest of the picture. About my age, thirty-something. Money to spend. Used to attention.

At this point, it was hard to tell if I was pretending to be flattered, or if I really was. I wondered what Johnny Renza's girlfriend looked like. When had she stopped feeling flattered? Was it when he started pressing her for pictures? Or maybe she didn't have a problem with it, at all. Maybe jealous Johnny was the one.

"How many more times can I come back before I decide?"

"You tell me."

"Can I bring a friend?" It would be Vicky, definitely Vicky.

"She look like you?"

"No, and neither does her fiancé."

He didn't bat an eye. "I'm here Mondays and Wednesdays. And Thursdays. Come on in." Before I could ask where he was the rest of the time, he was at the other end of the gym over by the massage chairs and the tanning rooms, talking up a couple of Wallpaper Twinkies who'd be old enough to order their high school rings in about three years. He never looked back.

The guy was, well, interesting. Not just because he was good looking, confident, even arrogant. There was something else about him. Attitude. Tons of stuff going on under the surface. I probably should have run a check on him before I went over, but sometimes an unbiased first impression works better. And here it comes. He's... a Player in the classic sense. Everything he does, everything he says, is intended to achieve the specific end, whatever it is, that gives him that smile.

Now, to find out what his game is.

# CHAPTER SIX

## Objects are closer than they appear

"Maybe he just has a thing for Renza's girlfriend," Tango Daly suggested. I was at Iroquois Investigations to work up some background on Lamar Jackson. "What does she look like?"

"Don't know. But I do know Renza, and he doesn't date anybody who couldn't be Miss November."

As soon as I said it, we had the same unfortunate thought. That *he'd dated me*. And I was no Miss November, although my 38DD's could be. But for that to happen, they couldn't be attached to the rest of me, with my acutely curly red hair, and my wide wheelbase and all the cushioning that came with it. Those Miss Whatever contest winners had no fat on their bodies at all, and would sink like a rock if they fell in a pool. But then, you can install all kinds of hidden flotation devices, can't you.

I dropped my purse on the floor somewhere near my desk and fired up the PC. It was an ancient Sony VAIO, and I was used to it. Daly understood this, and didn't pressure me to let him plant something fancier in my space, something that would boot up in our lifetime. He used the time to appraise me, which made me feel supremely self conscious, and irrationally excited.

Excited because Tango Daly – or whatever his real name was, "Tango" having come from his time in Special Forces doing things I might not want to know about – was that elusive and irresistible male combination of brains, experience, sensitivity, loyalty, clothes sense, and a natural physique that would have Michaelangelo's David weeping with envy. All of him.

Daly went back to the case he was working. The man had a knack for looking at ease while he was busting his ass. Nothing was too difficult; everything got done. Even the furniture cooperated. His leather desk chair was so comfortable, he could spend the night in it. It went with everything else about his office that was luxurious. The rich draperies, the thick carpet, the substantial mahogany desk, the fact that practically everything you saw was really something else.

A framed landscape could be a gun safe. Or fireproof document files. Or sets of buttons that initiated things you only read about in spy novels. A door that might ordinarily lead to a closet could go somewhere else entirely. At Iroquois, which is housed in a building that does not share a common wall with anybody else, the door takes you to a second floor outfitted with everything you'd need to carry on extended covert activity from a private location. Electronics, meals, plumbing, silky bedding and other essentials like champagne and caviar, should the need arise. And it has.

I try to keep my head on straight about Daly. There's nothing I'm not crazy about. He even took a big chance recently, telling me that he cared. Which is a problem for me, since getting tangled up in a relationship is the last thing on my list.

I'm not one of those women who "needs to focus on her work" to the exclusion of everything else. It's not like I'm doing scientific research, although even Marie Curie did have Pierre. I just do what I do, and Daly's always involved, and that's good enough. I'm just not a white-picket-fence-with-kiddies-in-the-yard kind of woman. Which drives my mother insane. The conversation plays out the same way every single time, at least once a month.

"Where are my grandchildren?" Ma demands to know, always at dinner, and somewhere between the end of the meat and the *gelato.*

"Talk to your handsome son Tony about that."

Tony's mouth is full of beef and his eyes are like saucers, shooting me the classic sibling alarm look, mouthing "Noooooo!"

Ma turns to me for round two. "You were married once, sure it was short, but what went on there?"

"Let us review. He died *on me,* on our honeymoon! And then it turned out he'd been a jewel thief who left me with a big mess on my hands! Remember? What part of that would make me want to get married again?"

"Sure, but that wasn't the only time you and he, you know. What's your plan? Are you going to adopt?"

"Ma, I'm not even married!"

At this point, Pop reaches down and hooks his index finger through the glass ring on the gallon of Gallo that's always on the floor by his chair, at the end of the table. Pouring for the family is his thing. "Who wants more?" Every face bears a different expression, a carousel of ideas rolling like a freight train through brains connected by DNA. *"Who needs more?"* as he fills his own glass to the rim.

I pulled myself out of that daydream and punched Lamar Jackson's name into the computer, hoping to find a solid resume' as appealing as his looks, and no problems whatsoever. Oh, the satisfaction of going to Renza and telling him his girlfriend's attraction to somebody else was all on the up and up, the guy was fine, even great, and such is life, it'll pass. Or not. Heh heh.

Instead, the actual facts in the readout on Jackson in no way represented him as he was marketing himself. On Facebook, for instance, he was Boston College; the prestigious Samuel T. Harding Award for Excellence in Physical Education, presented by Samuel T. Harding himself; associate degree in photojournalism from Centennial University School somewhere in Nevada. Volunteer work with "various youth groups".

The truth was, he had attended but hadn't graduated from high school. No big deal, maybe he had to quit to support his family. But Boston College didn't know who he was; there was no Samuel T. Harding award anywhere for anything, in fact there was no Samuel T. Harding, and so on. The volunteer work with youth groups, I didn't want to think about.

Address history for the past four years: average one every five weeks. He had used his current apartment address for the last nine months, and during that time had logged ten cell phone numbers, counting only the traceable ones in his name.

No outstanding warrants or even unpaid parking tickets. But he did have a slew of speeding citations, and guilty pleas to reckless driving charges over a period of years. These might not send up flashing red lights to an investigator, but I've found they're an accurate look into a person's attitude about authority in general, a kind of "fuck you" to any sort of rules and regs. Uncooperative and uncontrollable. Noted.

Work history: One other gym in Buffalo, which I confirmed. No problems. He told them he was leaving for a better offer. Presumably Kettlebells.

*Probable* associates: Four names, all male, all employed by Kettlebells, which it turns out is part of a chain of businesses with training-associated names: *Barbells, Inc; Weights, Inc; Resistance, Inc; Strength, Inc; Booty, Inc; Bootay, Inc.*

*Possible* associates: Two female names, and I am not making this up: Bunny Splash and Teddy Bare.

"Not again!" I shouted at Daly. "Oh no, not again! I swear, no more strippers! No more sweaty bouncers in putrid black wool jackets! No more backstage bloodlust! No, no more glass... my neck..." The floor began moving.

Daly was on his feet and on his way.

"Okay. It's okay." This time it took a solid six minutes of his arms around me to steady the rocking. A lot had come down in the past few months. It could've ended very, very badly. "Log off and forget about it until morning," he said. "Tomorrow, go in as a client."

"I'll take Vicky with me. She'll have him so mixed up, if he has a story he won't be able to keep it straight."

"I'll do the in-depth criminal for you. The less you know, the more innocent you'll look." Then, just to be a smartass, he whispered," And I do want a picture of that."

I jumped up and looked around for something to smack him with, which is my accustomed comeback to a pre-orchestrated insult; but before I could reach my hefty volume of Privacy Law, he had me by the wrist.

It made my day.

Grinning. Hazel eyes dancing. Languidly running his other hand through close-cropped hair like it was no big deal. So I went for a slap, not too hard, just to make a statement. He blocked it and held my arm tight. And looked at the floor in astonishment.

"I believe this is the first time I've seen you here in running shoes." His point was, the thick carpet trapped my stilettos on a regular basis, and that was part of the fun. I always wore something fabulous that didn't mind being noticed, not this yoga stuff. "You could get away, if you wanted."

"That's unfair. You know I have a weakness for medium weight silk," I said, imagining the creamy feel of his short sleeve shirt, "and summer wool Italian slacks." He shifted and the fabric moved slightly, unsure of where to lie on his fine, solid legs.

After a long moment of memory and of calculation, we relaxed into an unspoken truce. He let go of me, and my body begged him to reconsider.

"So, what're you working on?" I leaned over his desk, and didn't know if it was because I wanted to stay close or because I really gave a damn about the case. Okay, both.

"It's a potentially very high profile society divorce. The wife, Morgan Rekler, wants her husband, Zane, followed. She wants this because she thinks he's having her followed. They're nursing a pretty deep distrust of each other, but until now nobody has done anything about it. At least as far as she knows."

"Oh really? I get nervous when a woman wants a man's story dissected, but acts all sweet and innocent about it. I guarantee you she knows something or she's hiding something. I say this in spite of being a woman, and because of it."

"Right. It wouldn't be the first time an investigation at this agency was used as an alibi by the client."

"How can she keep acting as though nothing is wrong? If it were me, I wouldn't be able to hold it in."

"I asked her about that," he said, getting out his big yellow pad of notes. "No substantial answers, just a joke that will probably turn out to be the tip of the iceberg. When she bathes at night, she leaves her bath gloves to dry on the edge of the tub, where he'll see them first thing in the morning. She folds all the fingers and the thumb in, except for the middle finger. Good morning and fuck you."

# CHAPTER SEVEN

## Private heat

"She told you this? Very creative." I admired Morgan Rekler's style. "Did you have the debugging talk with her yet?"

"Coming up. Her husband must have had something substantial, some evidence to go on, before he sprung cash for an investigator. My guess is that he has cameras all over the house. With audio. Plug-ins with an endless power source. And real-time video on his mobile phone. And mini SD cards for backup."

"And his investigator, if there is one, could pop a GPS unit on her car and worry about the legalities later. Holy shit. What did she do to deserve all that?" I asked.

"This is where you come in," he said, handing me the file. "She's not telling me everything that could be important in a divorce case. She's leaving out a lot of her own background. For instance, Morgan Rekler was born Morgana Simms. Her mother was the controversial white witch, Bridget Simms."

"It says here she poisoned her lover."

In the newspaper article, Bridget looked frightened. It was hard to tell her age, and the write-up didn't say. Loose blonde hair past her shoulders, big eyes, wary, uncertain whether to smile. The writer said when Bridget walked, her long skirts whispered.

"Probably didn't poison him. The case faltered when her lawyer got the Assistant DA who was handling it, a guy named Redford Link, to admit he'd also handled Bridget, and that she'd left him when she found out he was married. Shortly thereafter, her new boyfriend turned up dead. It turned out, this boyfriend had been making the rounds when Bridget wasn't looking, so he left behind any number of women who wouldn't miss him. And who had the chance and a motive to get rid of him. She wasn't the only one."

Ouch. And I thought I had bad luck with men. Plus, I couldn't help wonder how you get it on hot 'n' heavy with a guy named Redford without laughing until you cry. *Oh Red, you're so hot! Do it to me, Red! Do it till I'm blue, Red!*

"How did it end?" I asked, always impatient for the bottom line, not finding anything particularly interesting on her daughter Morgan, so far.

"Bridget's lawyer had a cozy conversation with Link, suggesting some people might get the impression he was trying to frame her, out of revenge for being dumped."

"And so, suddenly he wasn't in the mood to go to court?"

"No, he wasn't. But his wife was, and that divorce case was one for the record books. Lots of unreported income on their joint tax returns. But more than that. Explosive stuff."

"How'd her lawyer find it?"

"The wife found it, herself. It was too easy. Link had bought an old barristers' desk. It was equipped with identical drawer configuration on both sides, because it had been designed for use by two people. This meant several extra keys were rolling around in the drawers. She suspected there was something funny about him, so she appropriated one of the keys and tucked it away like an insurance policy."

"And it paid off?"

"Big time. Link thought he was safe because he kept all the drawers locked. In his own house, he locked documents away from his wife. What he didn't know, was that when he was out making deals, bartering influence, collecting cash "protection money", she was home making copies of everything in the desk. Unfortunately, he was also very good at keeping coded records that other people couldn't read, so he was never prosecuted for serious crimes including conspiracy and accessory."

"Where is everybody now?" With my luck, a mind that treacherous would be Longoria's golfing buddy, what with protection money involved, and Longoria's influence on the job.

"Canada. Ontario. Still holding a grudge against Bridget. Link thinks he's hiding up there, but he's bad news, with too many ties in Buffalo for the rest of us to lose track of him. He does have ties to Longoria. And to wealthy individuals of influence.

So through her mother, Morgan Rekler had been exposed to turmoil. I opened her file again. The photo inside the cover was haunting. A candid shot. Frowning, alone at a café, uncomfortable. She and her mother looked very much alike. But Morgan's nonchalance, so irresistible to males and unsettling to females, was more polished. I supposed it came with marrying money.

42

*Are you like your mother? Have you learned not to trust men? Can you be trusted?*

"I can't do this job for her if she doesn't come clean," Daly said. "Whatever this is, it's not all in her husband's imagination. I'm going to need you to get to know her."

"Won't it be a little crowded out there? Madame X, then her husband, then you following him, then whoever is following her, then me... what am I doing again? It'll be like a Peter Sellers movie."

"Seriously, PJ. You and she don't travel in the same circles or have the same friends. She spells friends, and I don't think she has many of them, FRIEND$." He wrote it out with his finger on an imaginary blackboard in the air and drew a line down through the S. "I need you to manufacture a 'chance' meeting with her. It'll be difficult, because she doesn't go to the usual places for girl things. She has manicures at home, and somebody shows up to do her hair. She does have high-buck facials, and obviously gets exercise someplace. Shadow her for a couple of days and see where she goes."

"You mean, follow the guy who's following her." This could be really easy or really hard. Easy, if all I have to do is stick to the investigator who's shadowing her. Hard, if he knows it. Hard, if he can do his job and still concentrate on his rearview mirror.

"Speaking of dollar signs, I might need to buy a few things. Is there a budget for this?" I asked with the sweetest smile.

Daly pulled a roll of hundreds from his desk drawer and peeled off a few. "Keep me posted."

"You forgot your Baggies of meatballs!" Ma wailed into the phone. I'd called from the car to get a simple answer to a simple question. "You know you never leave here hungry. It's bad luck!" In the background, Nonna Giovanna was chanting something in Sicilian dialect, and it didn't sound happy. "See what you started?"

"Started? Started what?"

"Ever since that amulet came into the house! It's still sitting in the middle of the table. And then you left early!" Ma was talking to everybody at once. "*Signora Santini*, don't you dare light that rosemary. At least put a dish under it. Here, give it to me!" Chair legs were scraping the hardwood floor. "Dominic, take those damn matches away from your mother!"

"Put Pop on the phone!" The next sound I heard would be the voice of reason.

"Just another day here at Drama Central, little girl," he said. "I'm goin' down to the basement for something I can understand. We got a good lead on a missing teen."

"No, wait. What's going on?"

"Hard to say. Your Nonna's got a thing about that nothing little piece of jewelry you brought from Chickie. She doesn't like it. So I say I'll throw it out. God no, she says, not that! So I say, okay I won't throw it out, and she starts again."

"What's she saying? I mean, what's she saying most?"

"That if you make a mistake, you pay for it. Her exact words are 'Ama tella you an old Italian saying. Fuck up once, you lose two teeth.' I'm pretty sure she got that from a Mob movie."

"That's comforting. But what was the mistake, and who made it?"

"Who knows. Why'd you call?"

"I wanted to ask Ma who her friend is who works all the charity fundraisers. You know, the big dinners where people show up mostly to show off. People with money. The regulars. The silent auctions for luxury trips they can afford to take anyway, and autographed sports stuff."

"Oh, I can tell you that. It's Maria Powell."

"My mother knows somebody named Powell? It's the only person without a vowel at the end of her name."

"Maiden name: Puntadita. Ironic. Roughly translates to fingertip. In the real world, you have a cause and you want to raise money fast, Maria's got what you need. Right at her fingertips. I'm checkin' your mother's Rolodex for the number, as we speak."

"Would it be too much to ask if you could grab Ma in a quiet moment, and see if she'll make the call to Maria? Tell her just to find out if somebody named Morgan Rekler is ever involved in charity events, and where. She doesn't have to say why. But I need links to places Rekler might go."

"Why don't you just surveil her? She done something wrong?"

"She's a client." Which translated to *I can't tell you more.* "I think she's clean, I just need to know more about her."

"Okay, I'll do what I can." He paused, and the noise level behind him rose. "Quiet moment. You're kidding."

I let Pop go, to escape to the basement and await the next meal, a lunch that would come late but with plenty of entertainment.

Next call, Vicky.

*"Balducci's Love Your Dog,* ya got Vicky here!"

"How busy are you? What are you wearing?"

"What's this, an unsolicited sex call, the most fun I've had all day?"

"It's me, and you know it. I'm in a kind of a bind, and need for you to go someplace with me. Whatever you're wearing for work would be fine. Just please say you'll do it, and I'll tell you where to meet me."

"When have I ever said I wouldn't help? I love working cases with you. Besides, look at all the times you've returned the favor doing really difficult things to take some of the load off during my busiest grooming seasons. Like actually getting a leash and walking a dog... setting me up with some guy you met on a walk who owned a fleet of ice cream trucks... walking another dog... testifying in court that I knew nothing about his side business of selling ten-year-olds magazines on mail bombs and tactical gear..."

"Okay, I'm a little challenged in the dog grooming area. Walking is my specialty. So... what about today?"

"As it happens, I'm all caught up and Kerwood can finish the rest."

"Kerwood? The hairy kid with the runny nose?"

"Yeah, he's turning out to be really responsible with the dogs. He wants to be a vet. He even wears a dog collar."

"Vicky, he's a Goth. He graduated at the bottom of his class. The dogs like him because they think he's one of them."

⌒‿⌒

Twenty minutes later, we were in the self-park No Man's Land behind Kettlebells. I'm not exactly sure how to describe the way Vicky looked. There was nothing wrong with it. She could do a nice workout in the leggings and sneakers she wore to give dogs baths. She even smelled a little like the fancy perfume she sprayed on the Shih Tzus.

And she was in terrific shape, thanks to regular, take-no-prisoners roller derby matches. Her derby number **69** was tattooed on her deltoid, below a tiara speared with a bloody stiletto. This is a number a woman needs a lot of attitude to wear outside the rink, especially in Buffalo where everything has at least two meanings.

None of this was new, yet something about her was just... different. Ever since she and my cousin Sandro became an item, her appearance had changed ever so slightly, but continuously. If I'd known this was going to happen, I would have taken a head shot the first week and every week after that, then stapled them together into a flip picture book. You could flip forward, from no makeup to everything in the box. From flat, long blonde 60's hair to the Rocky Horror Picture Show. Or back, from Goodfellas to innocence personified. Something told me the evolution wasn't finished yet.

We hung out by the cars for a minute, while I filled her in on Lamar Jackson. Vicky would have him figured out right away.

We hiked up to the building, and a completely different pumped-up advertisement signed us in and summoned Lamar.

Lamar trotted over and caught up with us by the Leg Press.

He and Vicky sized each other up for a long moment. Then Vicky, the Mistress of Timing, removed her zip-up gym jacket with a flourish. Underneath was a low cut, lemony yellow sleeveless stretch top that said across the front, armpit to armpit, in black lettering so small you had to squint to read it: **These are not my eyes.**

# CHAPTER EIGHT

## *I know this guy...*

"I'll take your word for it, Miss Vicky," Lamar said smoothly, refocusing without missing a beat. "You been here before?"

A real cool customer. But clearly disarmed. They covered all the preliminaries and we got down to working the machines. After Vicky's quadriceps whipped through multiple sets of presses, and her glutes executed deep, meaningful squats that made me wish I'd stayed home, Lamar zoned out and spent some time contemplating the stitching on his bright orange shoes.

"Why are you here?" he said evenly, with much less enthusiasm. He didn't say it to me, it was obvious that I could use all the help I could get, but to Vicky. "Why? You don't need training. You probably are a trainer."

"I came with my friend. To help her get a feel for Kettlebells, that's all."

"Are you here to evaluate me? Or maybe find out something else in particular?" Chest out, chin down. A little too confrontational for a guy who makes a living counting sit-ups.

"I know my way around in here because roller derby is my passion, and I stay in shape for it."

Lamar frowned, deciding whether or not to believe her. In that moment's lull, the polished spot where his hair should be reminded me less of a benign coffee bean and more of the business end of something with a smooth full-metal jacket. It just came to me, one of those Italian flashes.

"Why are you shaking your head no?" Vicky asked me.

"I'm not."

"Yes you are."

"It's nothing."

Lamar might have decided he believed Vicky, because he went ahead and asked if we wanted to sign up.

"I don't really have time right now," I told him. "We'd like to come back tomorrow and do some more. What's good for you, Vicky, around two?" There hadn't been enough opportunity yet for him to get into showing off his pictures, if he were going to, and I needed to know if he would.

"Sorry, no can do. Fridays and Saturdays I'm at another location." He had recovered and was back to being flirty, flashing those teeth.

"Where? We can go there. This is really only beginning."

The smile faded. There was a lot going on behind the narrowed eyes.

"I don't think so," he said. "It's private."

"Where is it?"

"Masters Grand."

Masters Grand! This case had seemed like nothing. Now it

had potential, but there was a big ROAD BLOCKED sign in front of it, with flashing red lights. Getting in would be impossible, even if I got past the car jockeys.

My heart dropped through the floor, as my blood pressure shot through the roof. My right eyelid hadn't twitched like this since ninth grade, when I had to stand in front of the whole English class and read a paper I'd written on pork. Don't ask.

Always an A student in English, I'd bragged to the popular kids that I was going to ace it. They had copies so they could read along. There was a lot of snickering when the teacher stopped me and gave me a D on the spot, because she'd never seen anybody write "bacon" with a silent L sixteen times.

Vicky hustled me out into the parking lot.

"What's going on? What's the matter with you?"

"Masters Grand. I've been trying to figure out a way to get in there for years. Now I really want to, and I can't."

"Hmmm. Let me think on that."

I was just telling her not to mention it to Sandro – we wanted to walk in the front door in daylight, not tiptoe through broken glass in the back at night – when Ma called. She'd gotten in touch with Maria Powell.

It turned out Maria and Ma had been blood sisters ever since Ma's unfortunate arrest at St. Agatha's for running side bets at the church penny ante poker game. Actually, the arrest was for assaulting a police officer, which, depending on whom you asked, had been sort of an accident. But Maria was the brains behind the scheme, and Ma had never ratted her out. So Maria owed her one.

"Morgan Rekler is a very generous contributor to fundraisers for good causes," Ma said, "especially battered women's shelters and new-start programs. Everybody knows her, everybody likes her. Always making a donation or coming up with something for a silent auction. Jewelry, Hermès scarves.

"Of course," Ma wanted me to understand, "I would have no way of knowing that personally, since she doesn't know I exist, and I've never even held an Hermès scarf in my hands. Not ever. Not once." Pause. I didn't say anything, because I knew it was the run-up to... "Of course, Christmas is still coming, and who can say who might be grateful for this new flow of information."

"You're absolutely right, Ma. You deserve it. What's the rest?"

"Mrs. Rekler falls in love with expensive scarves, then falls out of love with them quicker than I can cook and clean and bring up two kids and try to understand what the hell your father's mother is trying to say at any given moment."

"I get it, Ma. I get it. I love you, we all love you. And we appreciate you. But Vicky and I are standing in a parking lot so hot my shoes are sticking to the pavement. Can you just tell me, are there any links to a particular location? Are her donations from anywhere besides a store?"

"Yes!" Ma loved delivering stories. "She just donated a golf club. An iron. Or a wood. Something she used to make some spectacular shot last spring, to win a big championship at her club."

"Which club?"

"The Masters Grand."

Oh, be still my foolish heart. "Masters Grand! Ma, you're the best! And what an investigator you are. Thank you!"

Now the Fates were baiting me. Two reasons to get into the place, and no way to do it. Vicky, who misses nothing, was drumming her fingers on the hood of the latest car Sandro gave her to "drive around for awhile", a red Ferrari. The engine was running and the A/C was spitting ice.

"I repeat," Vicky said, edging toward the door handle, "there may be a way. There are a lot of moving parts, so bear with me."

"Wait. Is it legal?"

"PJ! Such a question! He's legal and he likes you."

"Who?"

"Jordan McMeade. Remember him? Class president, very nice but socially slow, spent the entire second semester of senior year trying to figure out how to kiss. Graduated college Wienie Cum Laude. Very wealthy family. Two divorces already. But not because of his kissing, thank you, I got that job done."

"How do you know all this?"

"He came in to set up some boarding for his dogs next month. He wants to take his fiancée out on his grandfather's yacht. He said fiancée with a wink-wink nudge-nudge. Everybody with two weeks' tenure in the sack is now a fiancée."

"And?"

"He isn't married again, not yet. I didn't tell you, because you're so into Daly. And then, when you least expect it, you're back into Renza. I thought why complicate things. But he asked about you. How you are and what you're doing. Said he watches you on TV, and is really glad you didn't get killed in that My Apartment strip club thing."

"He said that?"

"Yeah. Maybe there's something there for you. Anyway, he belongs to Masters Grand, his whole family always has. Very upper upper."

At this point, my radar went up. "What does he do for a living now?" Hopefully nothing to do with the criminal justice system, speaking of complications.

"Nothing, I don't think."

"But a smart guy like him, his education would be wasted doing nothing."

"Let's let that be his problem. He's cuter now, he's filled out. And I always did like that he wasn't that impressed with his family's social standing." She saw I was thinking about it. "I repeat, Mas-ters Grand."

With Sandro away in Belleville to see his families – the one he was born into and the one he, um, acquired – Vicky and I would be free to have a cup of coffee with Jordan. She'd be straight with Sandro about it, telling him it had to do with a case I'm working, which wasn't a lie.

"Okay! Can you set it up? Let's see if we can get ourselves invited to the fancy place for a look around."

Vicky went back to work, and I'd had exercise clothes on for long enough I was sure my body would think some form of working out had taken place. So it must be time for a meal. Nobody would complain if I showed up looking like this at Aunt Fanny's Tea Room.

# CHAPTER NINE

## The ties that bind

Aunt Fanny's Tea Room had been in business in Buffalo, in one form or another, since City Hall was built in 1932. It owed its success to the fact that it was nowhere near City Hall. Or any Erie County government buildings. When politicians, lobbyists, and other folks who weren't supposed to be talking to each other wanted a place for an easy meal and conversation, they didn't walk down the street to a sandwich shop. Or go to a fancy restaurant with white tablecloths and lots of attention. They got in their cars and drove to Aunt Fanny's. It was, and it remains, a spot where you can show up in a suit or in a hardhat and get the same great home cookin' and the same treatment as everybody else. Aunt Fanny didn't give a rat's ass who you were, and her family still runs it with the same attitude.

Wooden block tables are situated in nooks and crannies, in this old house. Eating utensils are wrapped in paper napkins, and there's a pad and a pencil for you to check off your own menu choices from the printed list. You get your food pretty fast, but you know going in that it'll take however long it takes.

"Pick any table." A waiter in an apron that said *TEA WAS NEVER THE ISSUE* squeezed by with a loaded tray.

It was funny how some people insisted on wearing sunglasses the whole time they were there. Which only made everybody else curious about who they were and what they were doing. They must be cheating on a spouse or cheating on the taxpayer.

A newspaper reporter once stationed himself at a corner table with a view and did a surreptitious video. Then he went back to the office and isolated some very interesting still shots. He was aiming for the publication of a different black and white mystery photo each week, very Film Noir, when the whole thing blew up. Influential Buffalonians got wind of it and threatened never to speak to anyone from that paper ever again, not to mention the threat of a truckload of invasion of privacy lawsuits. So the idea was dumped.

I found a table even smaller than the rest, and wedged in to peruse the menu. The other nice thing about being here was that if I lost my mind and ordered Aunt Fanny's *Creamy Mashed Potatoes and Gravy,* and her *Secret Ingredient Hot Apple Pie with Pure Vanilla Ice Cream* so cold it hurt your teeth, no one I knew would be the wiser. Whether I had come with that in mind, I'd worry about later.

I filled out the menu slip the same way I shop on Amazon. Put lots of stuff in the cart, then go back and delete a few. So it was covered with checkmarks, and I couldn't bear erasing any of them. It was remarkably the same as being surprised when your handbag or your backpack is heavy. You empty and reload, clearing out mostly tissues and wrappers, and you still want everything that was inside before, so it's still just as heavy.

I was pondering this, when the harried waiter relieved me of all responsibility by whipping the order out of my hand on his way to the kitchen. He detoured at the front to greet somebody like an old friend.

Sandro. It was my cousin Sandro. Who was supposed to be in Belleville. I'd thought they called him "The Eel" only because of his shiny suits.

He swept the room a couple of times, and then he saw me.

"Yo! PJ!" In one smooth motion he advanced toward me pulling a chair away from another table and sat at mine, as if he'd been going to sit whether the chair had been there or not. "So. What brings you here."

"More to the point, what brings *you* here? You're supposed to be in Belleville!"

"Listen, we got a problem."

"We?"

"Family business."

"Whoa, hold it right there. You know I've always been grateful for the calls you make, getting me, shall we say, otherwise unavailable information. And teaching me stuff. Would this be about payback? Not complaining, just asking."

"Yes. And no."

Holy mother of pearl! What did he want me to do, kill somebody? Break their knee? Deliver a message with a .380 round? The paper napkin was coming apart on my nose as it soaked off the sweat. Different scenarios, none of them good, swam before me.

I imagined myself in a trench coat screwing a silencer on

Daisy, who would never be a party to that. Taking aim at a fuzzy figure getting out of a limo. In front of an Italian restaurant. *They want to use me because I am unknown to the Conglomerate and don't look like a person who would do that, and I won't arouse suspicion. But a trench coat in the summer? Epaulets or no epaulets? Black heels, definitely. Short leather gloves, black to match the shoes?*

"*Basta!* Stop! You know better than that." Sandro snapped his fingers in front of my eyes like The Amazing Kreskin. "You're family. You owe me nothing. *Capice.*"

He never ended a question like a question. It was more like a statement. On him it sounded perfectly normal. I just never knew when he really was asking a question.

"Okay, thanks." This little episode had just taken five years off my life. "What, then?"

"Payback is a bitch. But it's a fact of life. This problem is this: a certain individual has felt for some time that he is entitled to something that he is not getting. He believes he is not getting it because another individual is keeping it from taking place. And that the entire situation is a life-destroying mistake."

"Do I know either of these individuals?" I said, dreading the answer.

"Yes.

"Which... one?"

"The individual who is not cooperating."

"For god's sake, who is it?"

"Giovanna Santini."

"Nonna? Get out. She keeps lots of things from happening, that's just her. Next to retribution, protection is her strong suit, around the ole fiery cauldron. But what's this about?"

The waiter brought the food. It wouldn't all fit on the table, so Sandro made an executive decision. "We'll keep the potatoes. Keep the pie, the extra gravy, the butter, the bread, the turkey slices, the fried fish. Take away everything else and bring us a carafe of house red with two straws."

"It's that bad?" I asked Sandro.

"That bad."

"Waiter, hold it. Don't bring two straws. Bring two carafes."

Sandro is normally very cool. To get this worked up, to come back from Belleville early and have it be about "family business" that included the Santinis, well, he didn't say it, but I was worried his neck could be on the line.

The story Sandro told was too bizarre not to be true.

"Allow me to preface this by saying that however warm and fuzzy it might seem now, it potentially involves the New York and New Jersey families who can barely keep relations from going to shit on a good day. This goes back for years, and will go on for years. You don't want to get caught up in the middle of it."

"Hold on, wait a minute! This is pretty extreme. What's the matter, does Jersey not like the way New York people mow their lawn? What, do they want a new pattern? What's it got to do with us?"

"I'll try to keep it simple." We both emptied our glasses. "It started decades ago in Sicily when a beautiful sixteen-year-old girl called Giovanna Maria Mangana was really ripe, know what I mean."

"Easy, that's Nonna Giovanna you're talking about."

"Okay, let's say she was on the brink of womanhood, *Capice*. How am I doin." Without waiting for an answer, he went on.

"Giovanna had a thing for – dare I say a thing *with* – a wild boy, a real rebel on the next mountain over, named Massimo Serpa. They made a cute couple; laughing, fighting, making up, laughing, fighting, making up. Both bull-headed but crazy in love. And older than their years. They were tight. They were so close they could wear the same sheets at the same time. And they did. Everybody agreed, at least in Giovanna Maria's village, that the two of them should get married, because they really did love each other and nobody wanted no surprises, you get that. So they set the date and called the caterer, so to speak. You catchin' all this."

"Right. Pass the gravy." The buttery fragrance was not lost on me. It was piping hot, and its richness wafted up into my face the way it had when I was six. Ma would catch me hanging over the gravy boat when she put the bowl of string beans on the table, and slap the back of my head, "Don't sneeze in it! Set the table!"

I told Sandro, "Go ahead, I'm listening. And so they got married."

"Yes. No. Almost. This is the part that could start World War III."

# CHAPTER TEN

## Please Stand By...We Are Experiencing Testical Difficulties

A<br>ll dressed up and ready to go, Giovanna Maria waited at the altar of the tiny chapel. And waited. A girl resplendent in white, right down to her heirloom wedding handkerchief, with flowers crowning the long, curly jet hair her mother had pulled into an elegant chignon. The sheerest fabric with a hand-embroidered border covered Giovanna's precious features until the moment her husband could lift his new wife's veil. She was nervous with anticipation, yet filled with majesty and purpose. And trust.

What could have happened to Massimo? Just the night before, the moon was their witness as they again pledged their devotion to each other. He couldn't bear to let her go.

Comes 10 a.m. the next day, no Massimo. Also, no explanation.

"What, not even a note?" I stopped chewing. "C'mon, Sandro."

"Take it easy," he said as he shot his cuffs and buttered up some bread. "I am endeavoring to paint a picture, here."

So the young priest's smile faded as he stood motionless in his fine vestments, making the Sign of the Cross over and over, expecting to see Massimo come bounding through the arched wooden doors.

"The priest was new?"

"Yep," Sandro said. "This was also *his* first wedding, and no one had taught him how to handle a cluster fuck."

Surprise in the chapel gave way to shock, which morphed into fear. Anything could have prevented the wedding! As the minutes ticked by, relatives on both sides of the aisle developed theories about what had gone wrong. The incense-laden air, once peaceful, now was roiling with insults and accusations.

From the groom's side came calls for intercession from an assortment of male Saints, and suggestions that Giovanna Maria had deliberately gotten herself knocked up, precipitating all this, as if she could have done it all alone. From the bride's side, threats of retaliation for Massimo's running out on his obligations, if in fact there were any.

Sandro took another bite of turkey.

"While it is true that Italians are adept at verbal communication, the word in Belleville is that both sides on this particular occasion felt the need to employ physical gestures thus far unseen in a place of worship. This caused the new padre and the altar boys to suck up all the sacramental wine they could get their hands on, even as the wedding guests were beating the crap out of each other."

"Bottom line, please?" Now that our Aunt Fanny's food supply had been exhausted, I was getting impatient.

"Bottom line: This girl's big wedding day was a disaster. So she did something to get back at Massimo, and apparently it worked."

"Did what?"

"She did the thing."

"What thing? Are you saying she put a curse on him?" That sounded exactly like Nonna, but I had no idea she'd started so young.

"Curse is such an ugly word. Call it an intention. Not only has he not found true love in his entire life – and the days are getting shorter – he hasn't even had a decent erection."

"Oh my god. Too much information."

"There's more. Years go by. Maybe just weeks, who knows, this is Italy. Massimo gets married for real. So does Giovanna – to your grandfather, your Pop's dad." I nodded. So far I was following.

"Here's the problem, cousin: Massimo did well enough to father a son. And that son, Vinny, now runs the show in a certain part of New Jersey. My part."

"He's *that* Vincent Serpa?"

"Yep. Stepped waaay up from Sicily."

"So what does that have to do with us?"

Sandro got out a pen and began sketching a little hangman game on a napkin. One word, six letters, his own rules. There was no winning. With every sentence, he drew more of the stick figure and of the answer. It went like this:

"Break down the facts:

-*The* Vincent Serpa blames Nonna for ruining his beloved papa's life and wants the curse lifted, **F.**

-Vincent Serpa is in New Jersey. He IS Jersey, **U.**

-I'm in Jersey, **C.**

-Nonna is in New York, **K.**

-I'm related to Nonna, and so are you, **E.**

-Up until now, that has been a good thing, **D**.

-But now the New York family could get involved, with Jersey having to ask a rare favor, when it does not want to ask a rare favor, especially for this. Favors are normally saved for big stuff, so New York would love New Jersey being in a 'situation'. But if New York did move in on Nonna and the Santinis to get her to cooperate, this wouldn't be a tiptoe through the tulips. It could be very bad. Add to this the fact that Longoria would have the perfect excuse to no-holds-barred take you apart. You get my drift." He put all the letters together and added **Twice**. He underlined **Twice**.

"Serpa's father swears there were extenuating circumstances, and that it was only for Nonna and her family's safety that he disappeared that day. Of course, she could not have known that, when she did whatever she did. Still, the fact remains Vincent Serpa is not happy with Nonna, and by extension, he is not happy with the rest of the Santinis, of which I am one."

What could they do to torture Nonna? Put her on a leash and walk her past Italian restaurants, make her look at other people's menus? Tie her down to a chair and make her watch Sebastian Maniscalco with her mouth taped so she couldn't finish the punchlines? Or would they break something...

At that exact moment, Sandro's cell phone vibrated and we both nearly upended the table.

"Yeah!" His eyes got so wide, I turned to see if somebody had pulled a knife. "So sorry, Mr. Serpa, I didn't know it was you. Yes. Yessir. New York will sit down, but I should keep it small and fix it myself." Sandro's thin goatee was dancing, but no sound was coming out. He was always so cocky, I'd never seen him like this. Finally, "Right, Mr. Serpa. Will do, sir."

I started gathering my things. "He obviously doesn't know Nonna. And I hope they never meet."

"Brace yourself. Massimo is visiting Mr. Serpa as we speak, and he's here for five more days. Father and son time. We're going to have to get everybody together to wrap it up."

"*Marrone!* We'd better get the hell over to Lovejoy to see what Nonna has to say. I don't even know how to start." I waved down the waiter and reached for my wallet.

"Forget about it. Your money's no good here."

"How's that?"

"I know a guy."

On the drive over, I gave Ma and Pop notice that Sandro and I were coming to talk to Nonna about a little misunderstanding with a guy named Massimo. It'd be a good idea to let her know that, and to get some *Strega* into her as soon as possible. I didn't go into detail because chaos was going to reign regardless, and it might as well happen all at once.

Some families prop themselves up on couches and over-stuffed chairs in the living room and have orderly "family meetings" where everybody sips iced tea and takes turns contributing to solve a problem. They are not Italian.

We were back at the dining table, and the amulet was still lurking in the center of it. Nobody touched it. On the way in, Sandro and I had a quick conversation. We decided that he should be the one to present the explosive set of facts. That would leave me free to crawl under the table and tie Nonna's shoelaces together. This would give him a chance to run for his life, while I caught her as she went down.

It turned out that wasn't necessary. She walked in word-lessly and took her usual chair. An unnatural calmness had come over her. Her limp hands lay folded on the table.

One giant thought-bubble rose from all of us and hung overhead like a cumulus cloud: "What the fuck?"

There was no point putting down food or wine yet, because already nobody had an appetite, not even Pop; plus, the walls had been freshly painted, and this thing could go either way. So we all just... sat.

"So, Nonna," Sandro broke the silence with a good deal of restraint, making an effort to find the right words, "I'll cut to the chase. Massimo Serpa sends you his best."

To Pop, he said, "Massimo was engaged to Nonna before she met your dear, departed father. Just to be clear."

Then back to Nonna, "He says he meant no disrespect when he ran out on you and left you at the altar, that he had no choice. It pained him and it still does. All these years he did not know where to find you. It turns out that his son, Vincent Serpa, with whom I am in business in New Jersey, has the re-sources to locate you, now that you are here in Buffalo. Massimo is visiting his son for the next five days, and wishes to meet with you to make things right. He also would like you to take away the curse. Please."

Our heads were exploding! This friendly table had become an unfamiliar minefield of thoughts detonating intermittently, and it was not safe to tiptoe through. So Nonna worked her way slowly around it, directing attention at each of us, begin-ning with me to her left. She gazed deeply, soulfully into our eyes, setting us up for what was coming next. I couldn't tell if it was hello or goodbye.

The room had never felt so empty. You could count the steady ticks of the pendulum on the wall clock that Tony and I had given our parents for their thirtieth wedding anniversary... constant, laboring, as if nothing had changed.

Finally, Nonna reached into the pocket of her dress.

"Hit the deck!" Tony yelled.

We all did. Chairs went flying! Ma fought off the natural urge to take the tablecloth down with her, remembering the bad luck amulet was on it. Tony, in his 100% cotton "What, no f***in' ziti?" T-shirt sailed a good five feet into the living room on the polished floor. I'd been sitting next to Nonna, and had thrown myself sideways and probably dislocated my left shoulder. Sandro vanished into the kitchen. Pop, ever the police officer, went down into a crouch and reached for a firearm that wasn't there. His gallon of Gallo rolled into a corner like a grenade. We all stopped breathing and waited, half expecting it to go off.

When it didn't, Pop was the first to peer over the tabletop. Nonna was still sitting there, fingering her piece of white cloth.

"Is that it?" Tony said from behind the couch. "I mean, are you okay?"

Nonna nodded yes, and we all limped to our places and put the furniture back together.

She pointed to the amulet Chickie had found, then carefully opened the fabric in her hand. When it was fully unfolded, she ironed it down carefully with her fingers. Lovingly. And moved it to the center of the table.

It was the other half of the gold piece.

# CHAPTER ELEVEN

## *Does this dress make me look fast?*

"I wasa one, *come se dice,* how do you say it, one hot property," Nonna began. "Like-a da girl with a basket onna da tomato paste can."

Tony stepped in to help. "I bet nobody looked hotter in a peasant blouse, eh, Nonna?"

"You betcha! Offa da shoulder. An' dis..." she gestured to the amulet, "inna one piece, onna nice slice o' thin leather around my neck. *Tra i miei* ...between my... gazongas."

She explained that the night before their wedding, she gave it to Massimo. But he broke it in half, symbolizing that each of them would always carry a part of the other's love. They would be whole only when they were together. The gold was beautiful then, an image of the priestess Medusa, a symbol of Sicily and a symbol of protection.

"When he didn't show, he broka my heart. He broka my heart on purpose. *Bastardo!* An' ama cursa his half-a da piece. For the rest of his life, may he never find love!" She switched to a deep, throaty register. "An' may his dick fall off."

"Well," Sandro said, "you got the first part right."

"Eh," Nonna shrugged, "nothing's *perfetto*."

We had to figure out a way to get her to the bargaining table with Massimo and Vinny. And it had to be fast, before the New York family stepped in.

It had not escaped my attention that my sworn enemy, Detective Frank Longoria, was affiliated with them. He'd like nothing better than to put the squeeze on Nonna by having me arrested on suspicion of whatever he could make stick for awhile. He could score a two-fer. So I tossed that in.

"Nonna," I said, "Massimo's son says his father had no choice, that he did it to protect you. Like the Medusa. You should hear him out. If he meant you no harm, then your curse was a mistake. It could backfire. Not only that, if anybody touches his half with their fingers, the curse could reverse and that person could inherit it! What about Chickie? This is dangerous!"

I pulled out everything I'd ever heard about Old Country lore, and a few things I just made up.

"Oh my god!" Ma gift-wrapped it to make it irresistible to Nonna. "You were stressing out about that just yesterday! Make a mistake, you said, somebody pays. There's a message here! For god's sake, for PJ's sake, for everybody's sake, *meet with the guy already!*"

Nonna shrugged, then nodded no, then shrugged, then nodded yes. That was more consideration than most decisions got in this household.

It was settled. Sandro would set it up. It would be soon. Pop made the closing statement.

"Let's eat."

That evening back at my condo, I collapsed on the sofa and wondered if I should be writing a novel about all this, or if everybody's family went through these gymnastics. I doubted it. Out of habit, and in no way actually hungry, I picked up the phone to order from *Wei To Go*. It was because General Tso's Chicken always had a soothing effect on me. Maybe when they took my call they rolled their eyes, it's her again, and automatically stirred Valium into the sauce.

Before I could pull up their number, Vicky called. Jordan McMeade would be pleased if we would join him for lunch tomorrow at Masters Grand. At one p.m., not noon. Very civilized of him.

Naturally, the big question was what to wear. I chose a little tangerine sleeveless summer sheathe, hemline just above the knee, lined and nicely tailored to show off the waist I was about to create with my new cream satin corset. I hoped strapping down my assets would make me look curvy in a classy way, not so blimpy that Goodyear would sue for copyright infringement. The shoes would be a pair of blush-colored open-toed Ferragamo four-inch heels with Vara bows. A lot of height, a lot of gravity issues. But it's been my experience that the more you pay for heels, the harder you try to make them work.

Vicky said she was going to have a surprise for me. She wasn't joking.

Sweet Boy, Vicky and I pulled up in front of Masters Grand fifteen minutes early. Two of the car hops I knew jogged over to say hi, and I tried my luck at explaining my legitimate reason for being there. They bought it.

I'd been worried Vicky would look, how can I say it, like she was there to pick up protection money. But she'd completely changed. In Ralph Lauren cream linen, everything was different. True, the shoes were bright red, but one does want a hint of color.

'I'm going to start calling you Vicky-Lite. You look great!"

"I always look great. Concentrate," she said, as heavy oak doors opened to a world of wealth and power.

Jordan McMeade was watching for us... at the end of a long, perilous walk over slick polished marble, through the foyer where members lolled in easy chairs nursing their second vodka and tonics of the day. Then three slick marble steps up. This was how our heels saw it.

We took our time and did okay until the end, when Vicky delivered the news under her breath.

"I'm pregnant," she said softly. "This time for real." And I lost my footing on the last step.

"Say what?"

Jordan offered his hand, gracious and calm, and caught me. Now, that was impressive. *Easy girl, remember why you're here!*

It was a beautiful, large room overlooking the golf green. Filled with light. And happy people. And the carefree anticipation that only expense accounts can bring.

She was right, he was a cutie. His zits were gone and he'd put on a couple of pounds. Healthy tan, manicured nails, Italian loafers, Navy sport coat, crisp white shirt. During my normal date evaluation process, I would have focused on whether or not he'd bought those things before the divorce, when he could still remember what money looked like. But in his family's case, that would not be an issue.

"You look beautiful," he said to me. "So glad you had the time today."

"It's our pleasure, Jordan, thanks for the invitation. There's so much to catch up on!" Which translated to *Where's the broad?* As we followed the maitre'd to the table, I double-checked his free hand to see if there was even a tan line where a wedding ring should be. He was clean.

"Imagine," he said when we sat, "with myriad pet sitters and doggie retreats around, I walked into Vicky's. We talked about you, and here we are. It's wonderful to see you again." And he meant it. Which made me feel guilty, because I'd come to see Masters Grand and find Morgan Rekler, not entirely about him.

Even filled with people, the dining room was quiet; quiet enough that you could carry on a normal conversation with all its nuances, and be heard. You could have an intimate experience over a meal, without even trying. Jordan clearly was used to this. Why was it such foreign territory to me? Because I dined so often Chez Santini, where it's every man for himself.

Lunch was absolutely fantastic. Cold lobster on Bibb lettuce, *Crème brûlée* for dessert and endless Champagne. Except for Vicky, who wasn't drinking in her new delicate condition. She'd also backed off the eyeliner and the hair spray, and the effect was absolutely transformative. It reminded me of that newspaper photo of Bridget Simms. She looked like a girl, and almost... vulnerable.

We made small talk, no pressure for more. With Jordan there was no verbal thrusting and parrying. No trick questions. This, I found completely disarming, almost endearing. Then, just as I was enjoying the vacation, he suggested we have coffee and go for a tour of the place. Which, of course, for me had been the whole point of it from the beginning.

"You mean...now? Over there across the lobby?" My shoes were terrified it'd take more than one cup of coffee to drown the champagne and create some stability.

"Hey, terrific!" Vicky gave me a *this is why we're here* look.

"Right. Could we make the coffee a double espresso, *per piacere?*"

"*Certo, bella Signorina Santini, subito.*"

I'd said 'please', and he'd answered 'Of course, beautiful Miss Santini, right away' in perfect Italian, and he hadn't had to stretch for it at all. I hated myself for wondering if Daly could speak Italian.

Twenty minutes later, we were walking a mostly carpeted route through the Masters Grand inner sanctum. The Men's and Ladies' Lounges were off limits, but we hit the other high spots: The Pro Shop. The Family Pro Shop. The Executive Offices. The Cocktail bar. The Ballroom. The Indoor Swimming pool, Jacuzzis, Spa. We picked our way through the bodies by the Outdoor Swimming pool and the Swim-up bar.

No Morgan Rekler. It would be too risky to mention her to Jordan. What if I created a fake connection to justify asking, and then she showed up? It'd be Game Over.

Just when it looked like this had taken us as far as it could, we reached a short hallway marked FITNESS.

"I saved the best for last. Look at this, ladies!"

He swung open the door to a gym the size of an aircraft hangar. Okay, maybe commuter aircraft, but extra-large.

"Wow! It didn't look this big from the outside!" we said to-gether. I didn't know how many members this place had, but they could throw simultaneous family reunions.

Every piece of workout equipment imaginable was here. It was unlikely you'd have to wait more than a couple of minutes for anything you needed. And whoever put it together got ex-tra points for presentation. Everybody color-codes their dumbbells; but these were categorized and stored on easy-glide shelves that delivered whatever you wanted smoothly and without hassle. You'd never break a nail. When you put them back down and they returned to storage, they were auto-matically spritzed with disinfectant and dried with warm air.

There was a lot of energy in the room, but the people were really well-behaved. TV screens were viewed with earphones only; for everybody else, there was low-key elevator music. So it was a surprise when the noise level escalated somewhere be-hind one of the tall Circuit machines in the corner.

"I told you," she was saying, "I just don't want to do it anymore."

"Nobody made you do it in the first place," he replied, keep-ing it low.

"I know. But it felt comfortable then, and it doesn't now."

"Give it time."

"But you ask more and more of me," she said. "It's much too fast."

"Don't you honestly think your world is bigger now, that this helps you to see another side of yourself?" He was working on staying calm.

"Just stop pushing. I'm not doing it any more!" Louder.

"It's my job to push, you little bitch! You sure liked it be-fore!"

We got there just as Morgan Rekler took a solid swing at Lamar Jackson, the flat of her hand catching him hard against the jaw.

# CHAPTER TWELVE

## Bad girl

"Morgan!" I blurted out.

Embarrassed, she burst into tears, scooped up her water bottle, and was gone into the Ladies Rest Room. I took off after her. It didn't matter who she was or what it was about, there was something intimidating going on. And the word "bitch" had come from a guy I was getting to like less and less.

She was bent over one of the sinks, hair hanging in her face, getting ready to heave whatever elegant lunch she'd ordered off the menu. My money was on the low calorie Cobb Salad, having not much to go on besides her mother's earthy lifestyle and her own social standards that didn't allow for much experimentation. She'd choose uncomplicated fresh organic apple strips, celery bland enough not to compete with the sweetness of the apple but willing to be chopped into submission for the sake of the recipe, along with enough mayonnaise to unobtrusively pull it all together, and walnuts only if she were in the mood to deviate from the original idea. Which it appeared she was.

My University at Buffalo freshman year drinking party training kicked in, and I guided her through a smooth transfer from sink to toilet, where I held back her hair and she finished the process. Yep, it was the Cobb. But it sure didn't smell so appealing.

At the sink, I gave her a wet cloth towel to wipe things down, and a thimbleful of mouthwash from one of those fancy little baskets to help erase memories.

We hadn't spoken. She assessed her image in the mirror, and I dug into my purse. "I have a some lipstick with me," I said into the glass.

She smiled. "It's okay. Do I know you?"

"Not really."

"But you knew my name."

"I must have seen your picture somewhere." Which wasn't a lie. The somewhere just happened to be my investigation folder. I was trying to get to know her, in order to do a good job for her. Nothing wrong with that.

"Are you okay? It looked to me like that guy Lamar was overstepping." *Easy, take it very easy,*

"You know Lamar? Who are you?" She had that frightened look, the sad one in her photo. It might not have been a coincidence that she made donations to abused women charities. I don't believe in coincidence.

I wanted to be straight with her, but Lamar was getting on my nerves and losing his charm by the minute, which meant he could be story material. So to keep things uncomplicated all around, I gave her the name I'd given him, and added a little truth:

"My friends call me PJ. Listen, all of this in here, it's our secret, okay? You don't have to worry. Women have to stick together."

"You're so right. Most of the time, for me, the women I could tell about things like this are the women I shouldn't tell. Like my mother. She would be super-defensive for me." Yes, Bridget the white witch, and her unhappy track record with men. How far would she go?

"Or people I know from here", she went on. "To be treated wrong, well, it's embarrassing, not something you want to get around. People think less of you. Like it's your fault. And like when you tell them, you've placed them in a difficult position... especially here. Nobody really says what they're thinking, here." She'd put herself back together, but I got the feeling she wasn't ready to leave.

"I know what you mean. Here's an idea, Morgan. I'm not a member. I'm here with Jordan McMeade and another friend. Why don't you and I get together for lunch or a glass of wine, sometime? We could just relax and talk. Privately."

"I'd love that!" She lit up. "When?"

I figured if we didn't make a date now, the moment would pass and it'd never happen. So I took a chance and tried to act spontaneous. "I don't know what your schedule is like, let me think. Today's Friday. I'm free all weekend..."

"Actually," she said, glancing at the stalls in the bathroom, realizing only then that someone else might be there, and finally seeing that no one was, "I could do it tomorrow."

"Sounds good. 12:30 okay? You name the place." She hesitated. "Well, it's officially down on my calendar, so no problem, just text me and I'l be there."

Back in the gym, Jordan was studying the far wall, wishing he weren't there. All he'd signed up for was lunch.

Lamar had dropped his folksy facade and sunk into a sullen scowl. He'd stuck around long enough to see how things turned out between Morgan and me... what she'd told me, how much I knew about what was going on. We never lost eye contact, and it struck me that intuition goes both ways. He knew I wasn't just a customer. He was worried now.

In truth, I knew absolutely nothing about him and could do nothing. In the absence of any facts, I just plain didn't like him, and wouldn't mind getting in his way.

By the time the Masters Grand car jockeys watched Sweet Boy's tail lights disappear down the long, tree-lined drive that would take Vicky and me back to Oliver St., a couple of things were clear. I pulled over before the turn to categorize them.

1) Morgan Rekler was emotionally shot, a victim of some kind of abuse.

2) Lamar Jackson was exactly the user I thought he was. At first, it seemed he and Morgan were having words over training, but it was much more serious.

3) Jordan McMeade was a classy guy, too classy to ask of me the questions he should have under the circumstances. He was the perfect host. And I wouldn't be opposed to going out with him, if he kept his promise and followed up with a phone call.

4) Vicky was officially pregnant. Because she said so, and because only a preoccupation with pregnancy would render her completely oblivious to the looks she got from club members as she strutted around Masters Grand in fire engine red

shoes wearing nothing but subdued designer elegance, attitude, and a huge honkin' **69** on her arm.

Still idling at the end of the driveway, I got out my phone and dialed Daly.

"You okay?" I asked Vicky while it was ringing.

"Oh sure, I'm fine. I just haven't told Sandro yet."

"Why on earth not?"

She sighed. "He's still in Belleville. I don't want to do it over the phone."

So Sandro had returned to Buffalo yesterday strictly on business, only to set things up with Nonna, and had flown right back to New Jersey to report to the Serpas.

Daly answered, and I ran through everything that had happened, including an encounter with Lamar Jackson, and all the reasons why I wouldn't have to tail Morgan Rekler.

"In fact, we're having lunch tomorrow." This blew him away.

"Damn, you're good. You know all those jokes I make about your shooting? I take them back." A famous Daly pause. "Most of them."

When Vicky was on her way home, I went to the biggest bookstore I could find, in search of a quick guide to a thing I knew was important to Morgan Rekler, so we could make small talk: Golf.

My knowledge of golf didn't extend past a quick course in college. In week two, the instructor took me aside.

"Maybe you should try something with a bigger ball," he

said. "Just go over there and hit this bucketful, then call it a day. In fact, call it a semester."

"But I can't get an F, not in my Freshman year!"

"Don't worry, I'm giving you a C. For concussion. The doctor at the campus clinic is keeping that kid you hit out of classes for a week."

On the way to the SPORTS section of books, I passed SELF HELP. Some call it SELF HELL, and they have a point.

"*When He Stops Loving You*". "*It's Not Me, It's You*". "*It's Not You, It's Me*". "*50 Things To Know Before You Say I Do*". "*100 Things To Know Before Divorce Court*". It'd be embarrassing if anybody saw me here. I was about to blow on through, when a small red and gold volume caught my eye. Actually, what caught it was the words Dirty and Sex together in the subtitle.

*Bad Girl Sex For You* promised a guaranteed, step-by-step guide to being even more fabulous and alluring. Things to say, things to do. Alone or with the victim of your choice. A new way to walk. A sexier way to talk. Perfectly normal, natural and legal. You say your sex life is good already? Dirty tricks aren't only for politics. You might want to pick up a few little battery-powered assistants. Some girls, the book said, even named theirs. Ma always taught me that if you got one good recipe out of a book, it was worth the price of the whole thing, money well spent. This struck me as basically the same thing.

So I forgot all about golf and scooped up the last copy of *Bad Girl Sex for You*, just for research. About the time I got it tucked against my body to conceal the title on the way to the register, I saw the security camera. So I held the book up with an engaging smile in case anyone was monitoring There was only a one percent chance of that happening anymore. But if somebody were, the alternative would be worse, getting arrested for shoplifting a sex manual. I'd never live it down.

At checkout, I also snagged a copy of *Yeah!,* my favorite weekly gossip rag. It is completely without socially redeeming value, and that's the fun of it. On my way home to an evening of forbidden reading, I plotted the menu: General Tso's Shrimp from *Wei To Go,* and Double Stuffed Oreos. And whatever wine was open. What could possibly go wrong?

At that moment, at the far end of the bookstore stock room, at a small desk with a 17" monitor displaying a collage of security camera angles, the chain-smoking eavesdropping cop from *First Watch* was leaning over a second monitor.

"Hold it," he told the manager. "Stop right there. Freeze it."

For a security camera, the picture quality was excellent. PJ Santini was holding up her personal copy of *Bad Girl Sex For You* with a huge smile aimed defiantly at the lens.

# CHAPTER THIRTEEN

## Business

The ad was for something called *FirstME!*, a whole array of sex toys with an outrageously classy presentation. And the benevolent message that there's a world of satisfying knowledge awaiting you. And the marketing idea that everybody's entitled.

It was tucked into the References and Resources section at the end of *Bad Girl Sex For You*, with a web address guaranteed to crash the site if every reader went there at the same time.

Mothers used to make sure their daughters were jettisoned into the adult world with a solid set of Not-Without-An-Engagement-Ring values, and a good cookbook. Now, I could see mothers slipping this into their daughters' backpacks on the way to college, with a little note that said, "Always remember you have options. You are your most valuable asset."

The website had elegant, straightforward photos of packaging and price, with details a click away. There was the **FirstME!* vibrating *Magic Missile*, sort of a small beginner's version, but you wouldn't know it by the name. Waterproof, always a plus. Rechargeable right off your laptop. Unobtrusive black. Innocent looking. A girl might even be able to slip one through Airport Security without blushing. And there was the U-shaped *FirstME! called Two For The Money. The images it evoked were mind-boggling and made my nose run. Then there was The Ring, the one with a rubber round thing attached, which should've been called *UsTOO! or *HimTOO!, but who am I to argue with the experts.

Best of all, a person could pick one up in a store and go through Self Checkout, and no one would be the wiser. A huge selling point. I wanted them all.

After lunch with Morgan Rekler, I'd go shopping.

Meanwhile, Bridget Simms was with her daughter, upstairs at the main house of the Tudor style Rekler estate, after Morgan returned from Masters Grand. She'd shown her mother the bruises Lamar Jackson had left on her arm, and had confided in her, little by little, telling her all of it.

"I just can't explain the excitement in the beginning! Feeling attractive, developed, sexual... seen that way by a pumped up stud who could take an interest in anybody, and he chose me."

"Well," Bridget said, "that's not all bad. Not being married would've been better."

"I know. But he appreciated me, and Zane never did, not like that. So when he asked if he could take a couple of pictures to show my progress, I said sure. Then, I don't know, it just automatically got racy."

"Clothes or no clothes?"

"Bikini bottom. Sometimes I covered my nipples with my hands."

"Ooookay. That's it?"

"Thong. Sort of string thong, string on both sides."

"My god. Not judging, just saying."

"Then the pictures turned into videos. But nothing hard-core."

"I can breathe again."

Then that stuff wasn't so new anymore, and she wanted to stop. Lamar turned ugly, threatened her with public exposure. Her first thought was how Zane would react, and it terrified her. So she continued, until she just couldn't do it anymore. That was when Lamar grabbed her in front of other people today and called her a bitch.

"There was a really wonderful woman who saw it and followed me into the Restroom to see if I was okay. I actually threw up. We're having lunch tomorrow. She was only at Masters Grand with a friend, so she isn't one of the "Chosen Ones", thank god."

Bridget had been Morgan's model of free womanhood since the day she was born, so Bridget understood completely.

And here they were in the elegant mansion that had at first made her daughter so happy, three stories of stucco and bay windows and servants, the house she now was struggling to leave. From the outside, the beautiful stone and brick appeared reassuringly solid and stable. On the inside, turmoil reigned as the marriage came unglued. Bridget was there to help Morgan pack a couple of suitcases; they'd made a reservation for her at *La Fuite*, a hotel way out of town that Zane hopefully had never heard of.

They were poised with the luggage on the second floor landing when Zane – who wasn't supposed to be home until tomorrow – arrived with visitors and they all rushed through the lobby and into his office, slamming the door. The shouting began immediately.

Morgan took off down the stairs with her overnight bag, and Bridget followed, gathering her skirts and snagging another suitcase. It occurred to both of them that upstairs might have been a safer place, or leaving altogether, but they wanted to hear what was going on. Hopefully they could leave undetected.

Someone had launched a blistering attack on Zane.

"Completely irresponsible bookkeeping! Exactly what kind of owner are you, anyway! Kettlebells has to look like any other health club, with regular billing. Even too much billing. That's what they all expect, too much billing!"

Morgan was in shock. "My husband owns Kettlebells?"

Then Lamar's familiar phrasing lambasted Zane for being uber-rigid and controlling, something Morgan knew all too well.

"Too much hands-on, man, too much control to let the damn plan work," Lamar was saying. "I'm the one they deal with, I'm the one who keeps the books, you just get the pretty results. You gotta give me more latitude, man. I know what I'm doing. These girls practically beg to be movie stars."

But Zane's attention was on something else. "The really big issue," he said, turning to the third man, "is this: *I personally don't give a shit, but don't you think someone will notice when a girl goes missing?*"

"She's a runaway. Nobody notices."

"I meant, when she goes missing from the gym, where they make the main connections with Lamar. They always come back to the gym. And what happens when a girl disappears from the host girl's house altogether? It's been months!"

"I keep telling you," the third man said, "no problem. When this happens, the host girl just tells her parents – tells them or else – that the visitor had to leave early."

Bridget put out a hand to steady herself. "It can't be. I know that voice," she whispered.

Lamar to the third man: "As long as we're all finally here together – and frankly, I don't know how the hell you even got back into the country, you know what I call you, The Missing Link – now that we're all in one place, let's talk money. Where the fuck is it? I do all the work, train the females in the gym, recruit them, get them into the system. You, Mr. Canada, aren't even here and you get paid off bigger. And *you*," now talking to Zane, "you're right here, pretendin' like you don't know me, never time to talk, but you got plenty of time to audition what I find to see if riding 'em is fun, to see if 'education' will pay off. *You*, in particular," he said as he shoved his index finger in Zane's face, "I... have... issues.... with!" And the windows shook.

Zane was not only losing the meeting, he was nose-to-nose with the muscular Lamar across his desk. "Back off, Lefty! We'll get it straight."

Morgan was coming unglued. "Zane... with those girls. I didn't know he even knew Lamar!"

"Shhhhh!" Bridget knew the danger. "Let's go."

"But that was Lamar Jackson, the one I told you about. I don't know who the guy with the New York accent is."

86

Bridget's angry exhale would have blown out the Olympic flame. "I will kill him," she said softly.

"No, Mom, he's not worth it."

"Not Lamar, the other one. You don't remember. He's Redford Link, the bastard who wanted me to do life for murder. And now he's hurting you. Hurry, we're leaving."

# CHAPTER FOURTEEN

## *Break*

Bridget continued to whisper to her shocked daughter, to keep her from speaking as she pushed her to the door.

"I kicked him to the curb when he lied about not being married, so then he skulked off to Canada to keep breaking the law from there. Pornography, transporting girls for sex, I'll bet the ones he grooms spend time in Canada. He will pay. Here, off we go."

They'd just rounded the big lobby table when chaos erupted behind closed doors. Zane could not control his fury. He let out a weight lifter's groan and raised a heavy, iron 36-inch twin-shade Tiffany floor lamp over his head, heaving it between the men. Its deafening hard landing into the office entrance blew open the French doors and sent chards of leaded glass in all directions. An irregular pattern of arrows shredded expensive Italian silk Benevento Lampshade Co.© wall sconces and penetrated windows, bookshelves, even a dog-eared copy of *How to Win Friends, Kick Ass and Influence*

*People,* which had been given to Zane as a last resort by a frustrated marriage counselor.

"You crazy!" Lamar shouted, a coward when push came to shove, taking refuge behind his chair. "You're gonna kill somebody! You fuck-in cra-zy!"

"I'm bleeding!" Link whimpered, digging a four-inch sliver of emerald green glass out of his arm. "You just missed my vein, you sonofabitch!"

"You're out!" Zane screamed. "You're gone! Both of you! *Get out!*"

All three burst into the lobby at once, skating on fragments of broken glass and splinters of wood, each of them consumed with the treachery at hand, and the rage they felt in return. So it took a moment for their brains to process what they saw: Morgan and Bridget on their way out, frozen in place. The two women had been listening. They had heard everything.

It occurred to Morgan that confronting them might not be the best idea, but the men were so angry with each other, maybe she had a chance. Most of all, she was tired of being afraid.

"What the hell is this about? What have you gotten me into?"

Lamar, still enraged, covered the twenty-foot distance in two paces and slugged her, knocking her to the floor. "That was easy, I shoulda done it before," he said still walking. Then he turned. "You breathe one word of anything you heard, and I'll hurt you. Right after I show the world what's really goin' on under that skirt."

It wasn't her husband who helped Morgan to her feet, it was Bridget, who ordered Lamar out. "Leave. Just leave!" And he did.

Zane and Redford stood transfixed. Those two bitches, now what? What should be done about them?

"How long has this been going on?" Morgan said, lost in the pain that was throbbing under the hand she held to her eye.

"Long enough to get pictures of you too, Princess." When Zane called her Princess, it always preceded the back of his hand. "If you're thinking of using any of this to get a divorce settlement you don't deserve, forget it. I can prove you've been seeing a man, and what you've been doing with him. The pictures, they're my insurance."

"You knew about this, with me and Lamar?"

"It was my idea."

"What kind of husband does that?"

"The kind that takes a hint. You and your ridiculous bath gloves."

"You know what, Zane, fuck it. I don't care who knows. I really don't. I'll use the photos myself, leak them in Tweets, act all embarrassed, I'll be the victim and you'll get what's coming to you."

"That, I doubt." He was becoming calm again, which meant he was planning his violence.

She quickly grabbed her suitcase. "I'll be back for the rest. C'mon, Mom."

"I'm right behind you. Go! Call me on the cell when you're settled in." She whispered the rest into Morgan's ear: "Whatever you do, don't come back. Just don't." A storm was gathering inside Bridget. She inhaled deeply, taking in everything, as if something might make a difference in the way things turned out.

She had no intention of simply walking away. She worked quickly. When she finally did head for the door, she glanced over her shoulder at Zane on the terrace.

# CHAPTER FIFTEEN

## The ecstasy and the agony

My false lashes normally flutter open around ten in the morning. But today was like Christmas, and I surrendered to it. At 7 a.m. All night long I'd been having dreams about going through Airport Security, with the TSA stopping me for "carrying sexual devices without a license". Everyone in line behind me at PreCheck was steamed because I was holding them up, and I should have been smarter.

"But I didn't know you needed a license!" I moaned out loud in my sleep.

"That's because these items are not intended for use by women. Men automatically know the rules."

Sure, this was only a dream, but it really pissed me off. I crawled out of bed and pulled at the drapes over the floor-to-ceiling windows that offered a mind-blowing view of the marina below, right at the edge of Lake Erie. When my eyes could focus, they'd see a beautiful day.

I didn't remember arriving in the kitchen, or putting consecutive capsules of high-test in the new Nespresso machine – my mother's gift of a classy glass percolator being too complicated for me first thing in the morning. By the time I'd knocked down the espressos and vibrated into the shower, I'd vowed to resolve the *FirstME!!* issue before lunchtime.

<hr />

The journey out to buy unmentionable recreational items is not an everyday occurrence for a kid from Lovejoy, and not to be taken lightly. What's the wardrobe for it? Stilettos could look a little too professional. Maybe jeans and a loose shirt, I thought, so as to escape notice if the place is raided while I'm there. But the ad said you could get *FirstME!* at big box stores that even carried children's toys. So I compromised and took the shoes down to kitten heels and wore a dress, but a dress that was hot pink with a sweetheart neckline, something I could feel good about in a mugshot.

The third store was the charm. The *Magic Missile* was waiting. It sat in a nice, refined cardboard box with swirls of pink that matched my dress, inside a clear plastic box with a hinged black lid. I tried and tried, and couldn't get the damn thing open. But I was going to scan it myself, so I'd deal with the box when I got home. With a hammer, if I had to. I was about to jump-start my libido into a whole new phase, and plastic wasn't going to get in the way.

The *Magic Missile* hid in my cart under a pile of sensible purchases like hair color and vitamins until I wheeled into Self Checkout. Everything went smoothly. Scanning, bagging, paying. With giddy visions of unknown sensory thrills churning in my mind, I lunged for the sliding glass doors. They parted without question, a big yellow happy face on each side giving me a knowing wink and powerful advice: Have A *Nice* Day!

Just then, the store's RFID anti-theft alarm system was triggered. It must have picked up something in my bags. Panic swelled in my chest. I knew it was the *Missile* in that plastic case. There was no way I was fishing it out for inspection.

"Ma'am! Ma'am!" a gangly teenager with purple hair and a lip piercing in an orange store vest called from behind, trying to pull my cart back into the store. "I have to see what's in your bags." He yanked it inside, I yanked it outside. Inside, outside. The door slid open and half-closed, open and half-closed. He pulled hard, I pulled harder. People stopped to look. To my credit, my smile never wavered.

"Kids!" I joked indulgently. "It's okay, son, I got it."

But the little bastard was relentless.

The only thing to do was to pull out the ultimate Santini weapon. Channeling Nonna was not for amateurs, and it was a tactic to be saved for emergencies. I drew myself to my full height – which even in kitten heels still gave him two inches on me – and implemented the Santini Eye Lock.

"Are you... talking... to ME?" I asked him, raising my eyes to execute The Lock. Only a master can escape The Lock.

"No ma'am," he gulped, "I don't guess I am."

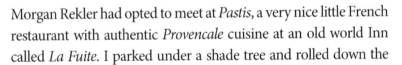

Morgan Rekler had opted to meet at *Pastis*, a very nice little French restaurant with authentic *Provencale* cuisine at an old world Inn called *La Fuite*. I parked under a shade tree and rolled down the windows to catch the breeze, and wait. Two minutes. Three.

"I hope this wasn't too much of a drive for you," she said, leaning in, and I about jumped out of my skin. "I don't know where you're coming from. It's just that the food is great here and we can talk, because it's nice and calm."

It's also at the other end of the world. Down a lane east of town, way east. First you're on the highway, then on the surface road, then off the map. It'd be a good place to have a clandestine affair, or hide out from the Mob. Which used to be a joke.

But that wasn't the point. I'd arrived early enough to watch her park and get out of the car. This speaks volumes about a person. For example, people who act unnaturally carefree can spend so much time choosing a space and arranging themselves when they climb out, that it's clear they are not entirely what they seem.

The point was, I was there early, yet I hadn't seen her arrive at all. Also I'm pretty good at minding the mirrors, and she absolutely had not been on the road behind me. Noted.

Inside it was cool and comfortable. Unlike Morgan, I'd left my sunglasses in the car and it took some time for the pupils to adjust to the lower light. A handful of tables already were occupied in the center of the small room, and Chintz draperies separated booths along the walls. Vintage lamps hung low. A movie set for a World War II spy story. And the exact opposite of the bright openness of Masters Grand. Here, even the act of ordering coffee would feel conspiratorial. I loved it.

We settled into a booth at the far end, and into our Bloody Marys. I decided to let her talk first. Which didn't happen the way I thought it would.

She sipped her drink a few times, said nothing, and finally lowered her sunglasses. Then she took them off entirely. The white of her right eye was an angry red. Blood was seeping purple into the swollen, perfect skin around it. There was a bruise on the side of her nose that I hadn't noticed before, almost covered with makeup.

"Oh my god! What the hell happened to you?"

She was right, this dining room was so quiet it ate sound, yet her whispers barely surfaced.

"He did it. He hit me." It wasn't crying, it was more of a whimper. Like a child whose feelings have been irreparably hurt, whose innocent trust has been crushed.

"Who?" and I held my breath for the answer.

"My husband. He hit me." She turned into the wall and began to sob.

"Morgan..." my heart was breaking for her, and I put my hand on her hand. "It'll be okay. It's okay." Of course it wasn't. It was completely fucked up, because she'd just confided in a person who hadn't even provided her real name. A person who was working for Daly, the investigator Morgan was paying to help her, to whom she would have shown this in the first place if she'd wanted him to know. If I told her who I really was now, she'd feel betrayed. And she'd already been betrayed once today. Or maybe last night. The bruise had settled in a bit.

"I can't go back," she said, "not now, not again. We were getting a divorce anyway, because he's not a good person. He scares me."

To be honest, it was a relief when my damn telephone rang while I was looking for the next thing to say to her, and couldn't find it. It was Daly.

"So so sorry, Morgan, if this weren't very important I wouldn't take it. Be right back," as I scampered to the front. There were people around, so I talked in code.

"Hey there. You know that issue we've been working on? I've got new information to share with the client's lawyers, and right now would be the time to do it."

"No, it wouldn't."

"Why not?"

"Because Zane Rekler is dead. He's been murdered."

# CHAPTER SIXTEEN

## *The night has a thousand lies*

Morgan was dabbing at her eyes with a napkin. I hadn't mentioned Zane.

"Shall I order another Bloody Mary?"

"Yes, please." She put the sunglasses back on.

This had become an interview, and it would be impossible to get the most out of it without seeing the subject's eyes, so I'd have to work around that. She was my client, whether or not she knew it, and this was my one chance to get immediate information that might help her, before the police found her and it would be too late.

"So when exactly did this happen?

"It doesn't matter, it's enough that it happened."

"Do you know what caused him... what's his name?... to do this to you?"

"My husband's name is Zane. We were just arguing. About nothing, about everything. As usual."

"And he just hit you."

She nodded.

"So, what happened after that?"

"I got away from him." New tears rolling down behind the glasses. "I wanted out, but he threatened to blackmail me..." the *me* trailing off in another sob.

"You wanted out of what?" I was pressing my luck, here, expecting an answer so soon. "Blackmail you with what?"

Deep sigh. "I wanted him to leave me alone, only that." Another sigh. "Pictures."

"Of you?"

"And him."

Long silences interrupted by long sips on our straws, until the ice started rattling around in the bottom.

"But how could your husband blackmail you over his own pictures? And if he's the one with the money, wouldn't he be blackmailing himself?"

No answer. Move on. By now the waitress was back with the second round, and it was a toss-up who needed them more.

"Would you ladies care to order lunch?" she asked the one of us who wasn't' crying.

"Keep 'em coming," I said, watching the door. Seconds were precious.

"So, Morgan, did you call the police?"

"God no, I don't need that. He's friends with them, anyway. He has lots of money. Everybody likes money."

"Friends with whom?" There are good cops, and there are... I didn't want to think about it.

"I don't know their names. I just see them around."

"Do you think he gives them money?"

"He gives everybody money. Even me." She thought about

it. "Of course, I'm the only one who couldn't get along with-out it."

"That's too bad. Does Zane tell you much about his busi-ness?"

"Nothing."

Then a slow smile broke as her lips parted and she mo-tioned for me to come closer. "But I know something he doesn't know. You see, once a week the jackass clips his finger-nails in the bathroom, over the nice granite counter between the twin sinks. Usually he throws the clippings away."

If she were Italian, I'd know exactly where this was going. Given that she grew up under the influence of a white witch, I'd say it was the same thing. Some women even scoop their clippings into their purses during manicures. Clippings are said to be the best material to use to cast a protection spell... or just the opposite.

"So you're saying usually he's very neat."

"No. I'm saying," she whispered as she checked for nosy lis-teners, "that stupid Zane pushed all his nail clippings together in a nice little pile, and forgot to throw them out. I got up in the morning and walked into the bathroom and saw them just sitting there, and I knew they were a gift from the Universe. So I wrapped them in Kleenex and stuffed them into a little inside pocket of my favorite *Louis Vuitton* shoulder bag. I would have put them in the zipper compartment, but that one is holding his desk keys."

She lifted out the straw, shook it off and tossed it, and knocked down the rest of the drink.

Inspired, I did the same thing – and then ordered two dou-ble espressos. Morgan might have been battered with Zane, and penniless without him, but she was not helpless. And she certainly was not stupid. Plus, she was the daughter of Bridget Simms who obviously had taught her a few things to do when the moon is full. As it happened, the moon was waxing toward full, the perfect time for healing and building. But not necessarily for evading the police or beating a murder rap. I needed to get the hell out of there fast, and talk with Daly.

"You're going to be okay, Morgan." This was not a certainty, but it sounded good. "You're a battered woman, and your face is messed up. If someone happened to see it and report it to the police, after all you're a high profile person, it wouldn't hurt to have a lawyer with you. And if there's anything personal you want to keep personal, put it someplace safe.

"Here, drink this espresso. Lots of sugar. This is an Inn, so you could stay here tonight if you wanted some extra time before all hell breaks loose. Sorry, but that's the truth. Do you have money for a room?"

"Yes."

"Do you have a lawyer?"

"Yes, from my mother."

"Is he good?"

"She's very, very good." Ah so, Bridget again. This would be the lawyer who represented Bridget in the murder case. It's not every day a defense attorney challenges a prosecutor who secretly happens to be her client's jealous former lover; and the client is charged, without decent physical evidence, with poisoning the new boyfriend. She was probably still writing it up in her memoirs.

"Then call this lawyer and be truthful with her, so she can help you. You'll be fine. Call me and let me know how you're doing. Please. I'll be thinking about you."

"And I'll be thinking about you," she smiled. "You're a good friend."

⌒

Right, a good friend. I felt like a heel. Everything I'd said had been aimed at helping her deal with whatever she was dealing with; but like Daly, even after our conversations I didn't know very much. I wanted to believe it all, but I could truly believe only what I could see: a black eye. And a woman who was genuinely hurting... about something.

This being Saturday, it seemed like a good time to stop by the TV station and leave a few notes to show I'd been there, without risking more involvement. The news director wouldn't be in, and assignments would be covered by the weekend reporters. Don't get me wrong, I love, love reporting. Today just wasn't the day for it.

From my office I dialed Daly back, and filled him in on Morgan's health and everything about our lunch. My entire nervous system had been on high alert ever since word that her husband had been murdered. It was only natural to try to reconcile her particular accounting of what had happened with this new development.

"So Daly. Details."

"Coroner puts the time of death at..."

"Already? It just happened!"

"Hold on. Coroner puts time of death at approximately 6:30 p.m. yesterday."

"You mean yesterday evening?"

"Exactly."

"But Morgan didn't know about it. She couldn't have known.

She didn't act like she knew. She just said she couldn't go back to her house after he hit her, and I figured it was this morning. I told her she could always spend the night at *La Fuite*, the Inn where we had lunch, until she could get her head together. And not to say anything to the police without a lawyer. She's going to use her mother's attorney."

"Interesting."

"How did he die? Are they sure it wasn't suicide or an accident?"

"Most people don't repeatedly bash their own skulls in with twenty-five pound dumbbells. This one was part of a set he kept out on the veranda off the family room, along with a treadmill and a big flat screen TV set to some business news channel."

"Ouch. Bashed in?"

"More than once."

"Morgan couldn't lift one of those."

"There's more. A contact at the Precinct says he could have taken the first blow, to the side of the head, while he was standing. He was 5'11". Either way, the second blow came when he was down."

"How do they know?"

"Trajectory."

"Which side?"

"Right. Why?"

"Just curious." Our client was in good physical shape, but that kind of sideward movement with a heavy object at that height would do some shoulder damage, and Morgan didn't have any. When I was getting out of the car, she impulsively reached up with both arms, without pain, to feel the smoothness of the shiny tree leaves overhanging the SLK. I remembered thinking she was just like Earth Mother Bridget.

"Get back to you with more later. Listen, PJ," Daly was shifting to his Protection Mode, like an alarm system or a German Shepherd. "I want you armed, all the time. Not that purse stuff. And, as we all know, not the ankle holster, after what happened in the strip club."

"It was the jeans. I don't wear those jeans anymore." They'd looked mindblowing, but had been so tight I couldn't raise my knee to access Daisy.

"Good decision."

"No decision. Can't zip them up." Damn. There went the kickass, sensuous, sort of Lauren Bacall in *To Have and Have Not* persona I'd tried so hard to cultivate with Daly. *What're you trying to do, guess her weight?*

"You have assets, babe, assets." Only he can end a conversation with a line other men use to try to start one. "Just one more thing. You know Homicide will be combing through all of Morgan's communication, and that will bring both of us into it. We have a right to do our work, but let's not give them too much. Why don't you call her on the landline at the Inn to see how she's doing."

So I did. "Morgan Rekler's room, please."

"I'm sorry, Ms. Rekler has checked out."

"But she just checked in!"

"No ma'am, she checked in yesterday afternoon at 3:30. No, sorry, that's when she made the reservation. She checked in at 8:00 p.m."

# CHAPTER SEVENTEEN

## *Pumped*

S he hadn't been straight with me. She'd already been staying at the Inn. To be fair, she never denied it. She also declined to say when she got the black eye. Obviously, there'd been a struggle. Maybe she'd made the hotel reservation because she planned to leave the bastard, and then he found out and everything went south. Maybe she hit him defensively with the dumbbell.... standing on a chair, using two hands... while he waited patiently for her to line up the shot. Not likely.

Or maybe she had a secret lover and the three of them had had it out, and the lover killed Zane. Then the lover took off for Mexico, and she stayed alone at the hotel, doing her nails and waiting for lunch with PJ the next day.

None of that worked.

It was a judgment call, whether the case Morgan Rekler had hired Iroquois Investigations to handle was over. She'd wanted us to tail her husband, but also to find out what made him tick. If what made him tick was beating up his wife, I couldn't just walk away from it. And if she were to face murder charges, she'd need all the information she could get. Or, her lawyer would.

On an uneventful Saturday in the newsroom, with only calls on the police scanner and our own occasional radio chatter breaking the silence, it was natural to let thoughts wander, to wish that something, anything, would make the case easier to understand. What had Zane been up to, and with whom?

I drew a diagram of all the people I knew who were involved. Morgan. Zane. Lamar Jackson. That was it.

No, wait. Johnny Renza's girlfriend knew Jackson, so that put her on the list, too. And Renza.

Then right on cue...

"Yo, Deadeye! What're you doing here?" It was Renza. Here at the station, at work, on a weekend. Looking killer, dressing the way he did in high school, only jacked up with stylish details for females who were older and would appreciate it. Jeans, of course, but short-sleeve powder blue linen on top and Sperry Topsiders on the ground. Damn.

"I could ask you the same question. What are you doing here? And I beg you, stop calling me Deadeye. I've developed an excellent aim since then, and the range reinstated my membership. Also, I don't use stick-on nails anymore."

"Just had a few things to tie up. How 'bout you? Anything come of that Kettlebells lead I gave you?" He was acting too nonchalant, as if it didn't matter. It made me wonder if I was doing his dirty work. I know that sounds uncharitable, but it's never been perfectly clear whether he turns on the charm just to benefit. As for showing up here just now, on more than one occasion he'd tailed me, for one reason or another.

"Lots of things have come of it. But tell me something. How's your girlfriend?"

"Why do you ask?"

"Just wondering. Is she still going to Kettlebells, still saving big on training?"

"Why do you ask?"

"Jesus, Johnny, what's the hell's the matter with you? Don't you get that what you're not saying is telling me everything? Trust me, it'll be better if you're straight with me."

He sat, looking very uncomfortable.

"Okay, she's not going anymore. It didn't work out."

"What about it didn't work out?"

"Her trainer, ole Lamar. Okay, I'm going to tell you something, but you can't use it. Can not use it. Understand? And, you have to keep it strictly between us."

"Okay," I told him, "I promise. What."

"They were just fooling around, you know, after hours, working out, oiling up, taking some pictures. First, pictures of them individually. Then together. Then the pictures turned to video. In a cell phone, it's only a matter of choosing a different icon and bingo, stills go to video."

"Holy shit. What was he doing with the pictures?"

"Well," he glanced into the hallway and closed the door, and I let him. "He was selling them."

"Did she get any money out of it?"

"Janice! Are you saying she did it for money?"

"Just asking, trying to get the picture."

"No, she didn't. She says she didn't. It was for kicks, it was fun and it was dangerous. Then she found out other people were seeing everything. Once in a database, always in a database, right?"

"So then what? She by any chance want out?"

"Did she ever. But when she told Lamar, he changed personalities completely, started shoving her around. Put bruises on her arm. He's very muscular, very strong."

"What did he tell her, to try to get her to stay?"

"That she was making her world bigger by letting herself go, with him, and by letting other people watch."

It was almost word for word what we'd overheard Lamar Jackson say to Morgan Rekler in the fitness room at Masters Grand.

"Did he threaten her in any way?"

"Well..." Renza started counting ceiling tiles, deciding what to tell me. "Manhandling her was threatening enough. But he also said he'd leak them to social media, with his own features camouflaged. That she could keep on doing what she was doing, or she could pay up, enough to cover lost revenue from clients who had their favorite girls to watch, and had paid in advance for subscriptions to see her."

I felt like throwing up. "By the way, did you actually see the bruises on your girlfriend's arm?"

"What, do you think I'm lying? Of course I did."

"Which arm was it?"

"Both of them."

How many other women were involved with Lamar? How many girls? Were the Twinkies over by the tanning machine meeting him after hours, too? Were they all present and accounted for?

And how'd he pull all that off in a commercial establishment... unless management knew about it and were complicit? How much money was coming in, and was it enough to make up for memberships that were never billed?

Note to myself: Daly can find out if Kettlebells is taking a loss on its income tax. Find out if creative bookkeeping has illegal dollars from pornography flowing through the business as legal membership fees. Pop: find out about the girls, on the off-chance there's a match for anybody who's turned up missing.

In Lovejoy, the clock was just striking Dinner Time and I was on the way. My internal calorie counter was spinning in anticipation. I'd tried telling Ma, "Just please give me a little lean meat and some salad," and you can imagine how that turned out.

"What, you don't like my cooking?"

"I love it. You know that. You just can't eat everything you want."

"Eat. People will think I don't feed you." That was Ma.

Nonna Giovanna was much more successful with guilt, and practiced economy with words.

"Shhht! Shhhht!" she'd exhale, and everything at the table would stop. "Do da right thing."

That was always the way it went, so I'd always eat. Bread and butter and oil. Today, there'd be Saturday ravioli. And heavenly, creamy dessert. If it's in front of you, are you going to turn it down? My dress was feeling tight already, and my stomach looked bigger, and I was still in the car.

To take my mind off of it, I worked out how much of the case I could share with Pop, and how much I could ask of him. It was very clear that it while Zane Rekler terrified his wife in some way, he hadn't been the one who had belted her on her right side. It was Lamar Jackson. Lefty. Charming, smooth, powerful Lamar, with the engaging smile and a gift for turning squats and lifts and tight bums into movie magic.

Morgan's story was woven with threads of truth from more than one drama. She had been struck, alright, and threatened with blackmail, but the big offender this time wasn't her husband. It was Lamar. So there were two men who'd brought relationships that seemed good at the time, and who she now wished would disappear.

One had disappeared, in a manner of speaking, but he continued to be a problem. Who, besides Morgan, hated him?

Just as I pulled up to the curb, Daly called.

"Hi Tango, I'm at the house, just going in to talk to Pop. I've got some things to tell you."

"And I've got some things for you. Our friend Zane Rekler was an investor who took lots of chances and pumped lots of money into his accounts. His best current performer is a corporation called Rekler NatureMade, Inc. The corporation markets diet supplements that the FDA is about to pull for false advertising; it backs chiropractors who run medical weight loss clinics illegally without doctors; and it owns upscale health clubs. Including..."

"Say it."

"*Kettlebells.*"

# CHAPTER EIGHTEEN

## Hook

"Kettlebells! Yes!" Did Rekler know Lamar Jackson? What was their relationship? Proof again that there's no such thing as coincidence. "What else?" I asked Daly, hanging back on the front lawn of the Santini funhouse, while I could still take a phone call without making it a group event.

"When they turned Rekler's body over, they found blood-soaked printouts of a very attractive blonde woman wearing nothing but baby oil. On a hip and thigh machine, arms and head thrown back in ecstasy, legs positioned in a gesture of welcome to the world."

"Oh my god. Morgan? Was it Morgan?"

"Yes."

"She wanted out. So did someone else, a friend of a friend. In both cases, the women were roughed up. And here's more: Morgan wasn't at the Inn when I called. She reserved a room at 3:30 yesterday afternoon, and arrived at 8:00 p.m. About an hour-and-a-half after her husband's death. She checked out after lunch today."

"You discussing any of this with your father?" Daly wanted to know.

"I will, some of it. I've got a hunch Lamar is using much younger females, too. He's very charismatic. I've seen him in action in the gym with the underage ones. Just a feeling. Pop might have some ideas from his Cold Case files."

"Let me know. And remember what I said about protecting yourself. We're getting closer to it, whatever it is."

"Do you worry about me?" Let's see him get out of that tease line.

"Parts of you."

"Touché."

Little did I know I was walking into a wind tunnel inside. The one-on-one I needed with Pop, the quiet information-gathering where nuance took the place of hard facts he might not be at liberty to share, wasn't going to happen.

Sandro had called the house with word that Vincent Serpa was bringing his father to Buffalo tomorrow, so that Massimo could meet with Nonna. The very same Nonna Giovanna who had recovered from her doldrums and now was in overdrive.

"Nonna, come sit down with me. We always sit here," Tony said soothingly, patting the seat of her chair at the table as she paced and panted, as if she were a nervous Poodle.

"Cunnilingus and psychiatry brought us to this!" she hissed.

"TV show again," Pop jumped in, lest anyone think that his mother actually knew what she'd just said.

"I can no do! *Sara' troppo.* Too much! Ama wanna take-a him apart."

"Mama, try to think of the family. Sandro. This isn't just about you and Massimo. That can't be changed. Whatever happens now is going to affect Sandro. And possibly all the rest of us." Pop was trying to be calm and logical and cool, but beads of sweat were forming across his brow. "Why is it that family crises always take more out of you than problems with strangers?"

"Too late! He'sa too late!" she declared over her shoulder as she galloped up the stairs. "Ama gonna sit on the *bidet*."

"But what about supper?" Pa wanted to know.

"I'm on the *bidet*! Start without me!"

But life wasn't complicated enough. Sandro had come into town early, and he and Vicky-Lite walked in the front door just as Ma was spooning out the marinated artichokes.

"Quiet!" we all whispered in unison. "She's upstairs cooling off!"

"I surmised as much," Sandro said as he pulled up chairs for Vicky and himself. "Hence, I thought it would be a good idea to prime her for the sit-down. Let her air her grievances in advance of Mr. Serpa's arrival."

He always sounded like a Mob movie, and today it was just too much for my father, who closed his eyes and crossed himself, pounding the table hard with his fist. And then it was over.

"In other words," I said, "you don't want her slapping the shit out of your boss, and going for a cleaver."

"Precisely. Am I not right, Vicky."

"Maybe this would be a good time for us to change the subject for a little while." Vicky put on a smile that nobody else was feeling. "We could chat while we eat, nothing heavy."

It was such a good idea, Ma gave her extra antipasto.

"Thanks, Mrs. Santini. I really need that, because I'm eating for two, now."

"For real? Congratulations! It'll be good to see some babies around here." Ma elbowed me. Her dig at me and Tony for not jumping into the game.

"Hey! Congratulations, you guys!" I acted like it was news to me, so Sandro didn't think he wasn't the first to find out. "But you never mentioned it. How'd it happen?"

"The usual way," Pop said, as he reached for the food.

"I mean, you're on the Pill, right?"

"Sure. Most of the time."

I rolled my eyes. If it could happen to her, it could happen to me.

"You know how it is, all the pressures of the dog business, all the solving crimes with you. Sometimes I forget things."

"Oh god. Well then, again, congratulations!"

"Thank you." Vicky adjusted herself in the chair, as if sitting had become more complicated. "We were getting married anyway, but I don't know exactly how this plays into it now."

"What do you mean? It's not like this sort of thing never happens." Tony, the relationship expert. "Some couples go years before they get married. Their little kids carry the flowers."

"I meant I wanted to wear white."

"You still can, no problem, " I said. "Especially since this is your first marriage."

Silence.

We all held our breaths.

"I said, this being your first marriage."

"Almost."

"Almost what?" I asked.

"Almost the first time."

"What's this, Twenty Questions? The answer is either yes or no." That was Pop. As a retired cop who had heard it all, he liked to get right to the point. More importantly, he had very little patience with conversation that might interfere with dinner. And the fragrant Italian red sauce that was bubbling on the stove required attention in the home stretch.

"The answer is no, of course," I said, to speed things up. "As we've known each other all our lives and you've hardly been out of my sight, I'm pretty sure you were never married before."

"Okay, I knew this would happen eventually. The answer's yes. But just once. And it was in Canada. So it doesn't count. Also, you didn't love him at the time."

# CHAPTER NINETEEN

## Red flag

"What?!" we all shouted in unison. "*Who? When?*"

"Senior year. Drinkin' beer with one of our good lookin' classmates in the rec room. You know, one of those Saturday night things at home that made our parents feel all warm and fuzzy and in control. We thought it'd be a hoot to drive fifteen minutes across the Peace Bridge to Canada and get married in this little hole-in-the-wall where you could do it on the spot. A sort of Justice of the Peace."

"Who was it? *Who*? Why didn't you tell me?" I thought I knew everything about Vicky. "Is he still in Buffalo?"

"No. Yes. I didn't want to upset you. You really liked him. We weren't dating or anything, we were just, well... he was so damn cute. Still is. You really had a thing for him."

I racked my brain, sifting through the list of guys I'd had a thing for. It was a long list. Of course, Johnny Renza was at the top. Always. So who was still in Buffalo, and who was still cute?

"Say it, just say it!"

"Some other time."

Being a female who hasn't had the best of luck with the opposite sex, the suspense was unbearable. I gave her the Italian eye, and she took a deep breath. Through a thick layer of her new, baby pink *Stick To Me* lip gloss, Vicky crooned the truth, doing an Eileen Brennan.

"Har-per Frasier."

Harper! My Harper! Of course, he didn't know he was My Harper, nobody did. We'd never even gone out, which I maintain is the reason we still talk to each other. I run into him all the time in Homicide at the Precinct. I'm a private detective, working for peanuts and the hottest boss on the planet. He's a paid detective, working for the creepiest, most corrupt, most dangerous Chief in history, Frank Longoria. We all grew up together in Lovejoy. Which means less to Longoria every day.

"Geez, let's move on, here," Pop said, preempting twenty more minutes of He said-She said. "Wear white. That's settled. Who wants wine?" He went to get the jug of Gallo. "She should start buying Drip Dry wedding dresses," he mumbled on his way into the kitchen.

"Are you mad at me? I mean, for not telling you? I swear nothing happened. If word had gotten out my mother woulda killed me." Vicky reached across the table and took my hand. "And look, were you not the first person to learn a certain update? Think about it. Still sisters?"

"It did knock the wind out of me. You know a person for years, and suddenly you find out there's been a big secret. That's not little, it's big." I had more to say, but Nonna was coming down the stairs. "I guess this isn't the time to look back. I'll forgive you now, and think about it later."

"Forgiva for what? She's a gooda girl. Notta like *some* people." She didn't expound on that, as we all were expected to know she was talking about Massimo, the guy who'd had it all when he had her but threw it away, presumably for some bigger-breasted half-breed *Milanese* bleach blonde from *Napoli*.

And the evening went on pretty much like that. The meeting was set for 1:00 p.m. tomorrow at *Ristorante Sicilia,* a small Italian place on the edge of the neighborhood. When Nonna seemed calmer and it was more likely the sit-down wasn't going to turn into a showdown, I headed home.

Just before bed, in an effort to put everything serious away for the night so I could get a little sleep, I went on a health kick and poured a glass of fizzy water, and caught our "Saturday 11 o'clock Edition" newscast, the last ten minutes of it. There was a new regular feature by Johnny Renza, something he had neglected to mention when I asked why he was in on a weekend. What difference would it have made? Actually the piece was pretty funny.

He was standing in a field behind a dilapidated house with a couch on the ground out back, and a cross-dressing scarecrow off to the side. It had on women's underwear, a business tie, and horn rims. "Sometimes," he said, "one thing leads to another. Police will be called to investigate one crime, and they discover something else. Here's a good example."

The control room called up a woman's mugshot and took it full screen. It was hard to tell what she really looked like. If she washed her hair, it'd be a full three shades lighter. She had the kind of face that could go either way – the tiniest bit of makeup would change her completely. She looked bored, and her brows were saying, "Who, me?"

"This is Darcy MacInerny. She lives in the house behind me. Someone pretending to be a pizza delivery man called the cops on Darcy, alleging she beat him down with a one-by-four on the front porch, when he asked her to pay for a sixteen-inch "All Or Nothing" fully loaded House Special pie. When the police arrived, she voluntarily let them in and invited them to have a look around, pointing her lit cigar toward the kitchen. No pizza. But they did find something interesting on the counter. A plastic food storage container labeled DOPE. When they opened it, guess what was inside. Her sizable methamphetamine stash."

He had video of police leaving with the actual evidence. Two TV stations showed up, because monitoring the police radio pays off with good stuff, especially on the weekend.

"But here's the rest of the story. She's been charged not only with possession, but with possession with intent to distribute a controlled substance, because of what authorities found out here. They just aren't sure how to take it into custody. A whole field of what appears to be Darcy's DOPE."

The shot panned down, and the news photographer took a slow walk with the camera low, through the field, brushing aside leaves and stalks, to reveal small sealed bags of the same stuff that she'd been sampling inside, neatly fixed in the undergrowth a couple of inches off the ground.

Renza leaned into the shot and winked. "Hidden in plain sight. Think Darcy was set up?"

Okay, I had to admit that was cute. Laughter is the best medicine, and it eases your mind for rest.

Laughter, and the genuine silk nightgown I really needed to-night. And shoe dreams that had been pretty scarce lately. I couldn't understand why Napoleon Solo, who in my imagination, had given up being the clever, hot, perfect *Man From UNCLE* and had turned to shoe sales, in order to caress my feet and sell me expensive heels while I slept, had suddenly blown me off. We'd been together for months, ever since I fired that sexy George Clooney for letting his hair grow. Had Napoleon left me because I'd run out of bedtime champagne? I would buy some.

The Concierge downstairs woke me at 6:13 a.m.

"Buhboh...?"

"Miss PJ? That is you?"

"Buhboh...?"

"Miss PJ, is you Concierge. You have a visitor."

"Who?"

"Mr. Daly. I should send him up?"

If my life were a novel, who'd be writing it? It would have to be some unbalanced creature with no mercy for her characters, especially the heroine, and no concept of how much a person can take in a twenty-four hour period.

For months the new Concierge, Javier Calderon, who had come to us from his former employer, the ketchup factory, had let anyone and everyone come up to my condo. He did this without regard for, well, anything. He'd even accepted bribes to do it. Why now, at 6:13 a.m., should he suddenly become re-sponsible and capable of linear thinking?

"Send him up." I said that only because it was Tango, and be-cause he would never just show up unless it were really important.

I threw on the default fuzzy pink robe over the glamorous silk, because morning is no time to deviate from the tried and true.

The elevator dinged and I made it to the door in time to watch Daly through the peephole, entering the hallway and leaning against the wall like there was nothing going on. It was his specialty. When he finished, he grinned at me and I jumped. Of course he knew I was there.

"Catch you at a bad time?" he asked, scanning the living room for signs of life. "You're alone."

"Would I be wearing this if I weren't? It had better be good."

"It is. After this, you won't need coffee."

We settled at the dining room table, as there was no kitchen table nearer the coffee machine. He presented a legal size Manila envelope with one of those metal clasps. It said "PJ" on it.

"What's this?" I asked, barely able to sit upright.

"Not what. Who."

"Who, then."

"Morgan Rekler."

"Huh?"

"I don't know what's inside. I do know that I was napping upstairs at the office after a night of monitoring an industrial espionage case, when a call came in on the regular Iroquois Investigations line, and it was Morgan. She said she had to drop off something right away. As I was already there, I told her to come over. I met her at the front door, she gave me the envelope, she went away. I watched her on the security monitor, opening the door of a Mercedes C Class – rented, I checked the plate – and driving off. Two interesting things: 1) she was not in police custody, and 2) this has your name on it. I never told her you worked for Iroquois."

"I never told her, either."

# CHAPTER TWENTY

## Movement

was awake now, and feeling guilty and embarrassed. "What's in it?"

"I don't know. I don't open other people's mail. Coffee, anyway?"

"Yes, please."

Inside the envelope there was a note on heavy, watermarked *La Fuite* letterhead.

*Dear PJ, You said I should put my personal things some place safe. So I ask you to hold this for me. I saw you on TV. We didn't tell each other everything, and I misled you a little, but I still count you as a friend. Thank you. See you soon. Morgan*

This was flattering, but how good a friend? We hardly knew each other. It would have been nice to believe she wasn't deliberately making me an accessory to something. Worse, pinning an entire crime on me.

In a smaller, unsealed envelope, there were eighteen very compromising color photos of Morgan, some with Lamar Jackson. What was the girl thinking! She looked like she was having a pretty good time. Then she looked like she wasn't. There was also a sandwich-size Ziploc *Baggie* with two keys. One looked like a door key. The other, smaller, said *Weiser*. It went to a padlock. And a cocktail napkin from Masters Grand folded into a triangle, with five numbers scrawled in pink lip pencil: 35260.

"Could I be made to relinquish these things, and wind up implicating myself?" I asked Daly. I figured she hadn't been charged with anything, at least not yet. If she had, she probably wouldn't have been able to deliver envelopes to our office.

"Use your source."

So I called Pop. It's never too early to talk in the Santini household. Somebody was bound to be up, especially today.

"I know, Pop, you're asking yourself what I'm doing up. Probably shouldn't tell you. We didn't get to talk before, and I just have one question: Anybody charged in the Rekler death?"

"That would be a matter of public record. I have not gotten a call, so I'll say no."

"Just wondering. How's everything going with Nonna?"

"Hard to say. She's spending a lot of time on the new *bidet* toy, and nobody's complaining about her near-meditative state afterward. It has a setting that blows warm air. When it comes to jilted brides, apparently there's a correlation between the amount of hot air blowing up the bottom and the amount of it coming out the top."

"Good luck. I've got some things to take care of. See you about 12:45. Love you."

"You too, little girl.... Hey Mama, are you ever comin' out of there? There's only one shower, you know!"

⌒

Daly went home and I went into the bathroom to put myself together. For days like this when my brain was rattling around, I had a go-to battle plan. Printed it out myself. Laminated it, and stuck it on the wall.

Sonic toothbrush with timer: go from upper left, clockwise.
Neck up: hot rollers, face cream, under eye cover, mascara, lip liner, red lipstick.
Waist to knees: liberal amts Cellulite-Be-Gone.
Undies: strapless corset. Flesh-colored all around = no mistakes.
Clothes: one-piece anything, black goes with everything.
Legs: *cold weather, black opaque Wolford thigh-highs.
*warm weather, suntan sheer Wolford or bare legs.
Shoes: heels, heels, heels ♡

I chose a sleeveless black linen sheath, bare legs and strappy black Charles Jourdan heels. Understated and kick-ass Italian, which I thought the Serpas would appreciate. And what the hell, hoop earrings.

The whole time, I was thinking about Morgan's keys. Maybe they weren't hers. Were they Zane's? What did they open? I didn't want to push her, but was ready to take a chance and call her to find out. I about dropped the phone, because at that exact moment she was calling me.

"Hi PJ, did you get my envelope?"

"Yep, I have it right here. What would you like me to do with it?"

"Just keep it. This is confidential...you... me... Mr. Daly. I'm still... client. Use it if you have to."

"To do what?"

"...don't know. This is...uch bigger...important. Can't talk long... phone's ...power and I forgot...charger. Signal's terrible. The key..."

"What? I lost you. Say again."

Static. "...key...are..."

"Again! Say it again!"

"...ah...are....."

"Hello? Morgan? You there?"

Nothing.

Shit.

⌒

Nonna said she needed her family around her today, so she insisted her son and daughter-in-law and Tony and I all go with her on the short trip to *Sicilia*. All these years, I didn't know it was Mafia, although I'd had an idea. The one time Vicky and I tripped in for lunch, silly girls all dolled up and ready for nothing, things were not what they should have been. There was a lavish, full buffet the length of a train car; but the place was deserted except for one table of customers. Men. In the corner. Deep in discussion. The other clue would have been a waiter who was a Sandro clone, hastily folding a kitchen towel on his arm as he rushed to head us off at the front.

"What can I do for you ladies?"

"Well... are you open?" Vicky does wide-eyed really well.

"Sure. What would youze like?"

"Um, a menu?"

Nothing.

Please?"

"Only the buffet." Got it. We had the distinct impression we'd be in the way, so we said we'd come back some other time. We chose to take his grunt for, "Okay, and if there's ever anything we can do for you, please don't hesitate to ask. Thanks for stopping by."

So now, we were headed back to *Sicilia*. I doubted Ma and Pop had ever been there. When you live in an Italian restaurant and are convinced it's the best, what would be the point of paying to eat someplace else? We were about to pile into Pop's car, when Sandro and Vicky pulled up in a nice, big BMW X5.

"Get in!" Sandro said, jumping out and offering his arm to Nonna. He'd caught her when her brain was running two programs, toggling back and forth between tearful silence and professional grade vengeance, so she was easy to steer into the car. Then to Pop, he said, "Best to keep things separated, vehicle-wise."

My father, who would not want his personal car spotted at this establishment, nodded his thanks. So even he knew about *Sicilia;* but then, that was his job. I hoped it didn't get back to Daly that I'd been oblivious to it.

"Gotta ask, don't want to, but gotta ask." Sandro said to my father as he climbed in, "You heavy?"

Pop didn't look surprised, and he didn't hesitate. "No. Of course not."

# CHAPTER TWENTY-ONE

## Line

When we came to a stop in the gravel parking lot, Lurch from *The Addams Family* was waiting. Black suit and tie, white shirt. A face out of a train wreck. His hands were low over his privates, palm-over-knuckle, as if he'd come to pay his respects. He sized us up and took a long look at Sandro. Satisfied, he stepped aside. "Follow me."

Vincent Serpa, recognizable from all the news stories in his perfect double-breasted suit, but minus his lawyer, was sitting at the corner table with his father. Massimo gave a start when he looked up and spotted Nonna. Was it the shock of what the passage of time had done to her? Or did she look fetching in the new black lace she'd casually draped over her long sleeve dress in this summer heat? Or was he worried how he must look, with his head of thick white hair and seasons of sun showing on his face? Or, and I hoped this was most true, was he moved to be in close proximity, again, to the girl he had loved so deeply?

"It's nice to see all you good people. Thank you for coming," Serpa said, standing to greet us. He didn't offer his hand, but in his world the Boss's standing was enough to show respect. I thought later that he had, of course, known as much about us as anybody did, including Pop's background, and he had been gentleman enough not to put Pop – to put them both – in an awkward position on this important occasion for his father. Or maybe he'd put his information about Nonna to work, including the time she set a ritual bonfire the size of a Buick on the front lawn, and decided the last thing he wanted was for her to leave more pissed off than when she got there.

Massimo had struggled to his feet, waving off his son's help, and never taking his eyes off Giovanna Maria. He was a good foot taller. A nice white summer shirt, cut the Italian way, hugged his chest. Sleeves rolled precisely to just below the elbow. Even in his advanced age he was living up to his name: Maximum. Wowza! Charisma, the real thing. No wonder they hadn't been able to keep their hands off each other. And at that young age, they'd both still been dealing with just the raw material.

It was a round table, always a good idea. No right, no left, which meant no right, no wrong. Introductions all around. Nonna was flanked by Pop on one side, and Sandro on the other, the theory being that if she made a lunge for anybody, either of them could do the tackle.

Massimo put his hand on his heart and bowed gently to Nonna in a gesture of greeting that seemed to the rest of us an intimacy between them. It was very endearing.

*Oh dear god. When he's looking down, please don't let her crack his head with a wine bottle.*

As if rehearsed, they eased down to their chairs at the same time. A tenderness had settled into Nonna's expression that might have been reserved for him alone. And yet, I sensed there was a part of herself she'd never give up. This time when she reached into her pocket, nobody jumped except Vincent Serpa's bodyguard. She brought out the embroidered white handkerchief she'd been carrying on their wedding day and slid it across the tablecloth to the center, so everyone could see what was inside.

Massimo immediately teared up. He saw that she still had her amulet, *had* had it, had kept it dear, through all the years she'd been married, through Pop's father's death, until this very day. But he did not have his. He remembered their promise when they were lovers, "*Per sempre significa per sempre*". Forever means forever.

In the hustle of leaving the house, I'd stayed behind to place Massimo's half of the amulet in an envelope, to bring it along. I didn't touch it, just to be on the safe side, not in the mood for second-hand curses. Now was the time to release it a few inches away from him. It wasn't up to me to put them together. It could mean too many things to too many people, and I still had lots of living to do.

Massimo gasped and looked at his son. "*Ma che cosa?*" How could this be?

"It's alright, Papa, it's okay. It turned up."

To us: "We will speak English; it's faster, with fewer opportunities for misunderstanding. I will translate for my father.

"Are you sure about that, Mr. Serpa?" I said. "Nonna's English comes mostly from movies and television. There's so much room for misinterpretation, you could drive a Sicilian fishing boat through the pauses and nuances."

"We will chance it. Lunch, anyone? We have an exceptional meal, just over there."

He nodded toward the buffet Vicky and I had seen before, with everything from marinated sardines, tiny shrimps in *salsa rosa,* and grilled zucchini in olive oil, to insalata Caprese with buffalo *mozzarella,* fresh picked tomatoes and extra basil, classic cold zucchini blossom *frittata,* and green salad. The chef appeared with a tray of piping hot vertical eggplants and baked, stuffed *melanzana all' Etna.* With dessert later, it would be the perfect meal for an occasion, maybe a wedding. Hopefully this would not occur to Nonna. At any other time, given my frustration level, I would have been rolling around in it. Even Ma's nostrils were twitching. This was the most approval she could afford to show, without doing irreparable damage to her diva-in-the-kitchen reputation.

No one got up for the food. The spell had been cast. So we began.

Giovanna Maria and Massimo searched each other's eyes, as the rest of us held our breaths. Was it that each was unwilling to speak first, or were they uncertain of what to say?

Finally, it was Nonna, and we strained to hear her. She seemed small and very far away.

"*Where were you?* Ama wait. Ama wait for you. *For you, solomente tu.* Ama wait at da altar, Massimo. Ama wait at night. And the nexta day. And wherever, Ama wait every day *e* every night." She twisted her skirt fabric into knots. "Soma ting terrible had happen to you. But nobody would tell me nothing." She opened her hands to show they were empty. "*Niente.* Your own family, they say nothing. How could they lie to me, when they were in the chapel with me? Agony *per molti anni,* many years." Her face was wet with tears.

Now she kicked up the volume, and I gave her credit for

putting it off for as long as she had. I would have been crazed by now.

"*Where were you? Dopo tutti,* after all of this, Massimo, I see you now ina front of me. Ama glad you are alive, and well. *Ma sinceramente,* but really, that was not always true. And now you want me to take away the curse."

"Si."

"You don't, *come se dice,* you no flinch. You no afraid. Maybe you should be."

# CHAPTER TWENTY-TWO

## Again

Massimo didn't blink. The storm was building.

"To see you now! And to see you in front of me without *l'amuleto d'oro*, my Medusa, this breaka my heart. I kept my word, you did not. You did not *keep* it."

"But I did! I carried it with me until only a few days ago," Massimo said. "I confided in my son the despair I felt without you, never finding you, *believing you never wanted to be found*. Please understand, when I talk with Vincenzo about you, I talk of loving a woman before I met his mother. This is not easy."

"*Facile*? I'm glad it's not easy! For you it should be hard! And it should be the *only* thing about you that's hard!" Her tone fell and swelled like an angry sea until it reached aria range, and every male at the table instinctively put his hands on his pants.

Her fingers were forked as her arm reached for the stars, and we all expected her to lower it on Massimo. But she didn't do it.

"On your half of *l'amuleto* I putta curse. For what you did, you should never find happiness... in any way. Era *abbastanza*... enough." We all turned involuntarily to Vincent and shared the same thought: *Massimo had found happiness at least once.*

"I understand." The boss was not without a sense of humor. "And I know there's no right answer here." Serpa knew the odds of his father's winning this one were slim. "Pop, ya gotta give me something to work with, here." He managed a smile.

"*Carissima,*" Massimo pleaded, "please! I had no choice. To save you, I had to leave. Vanish. From you, even from my family. Please believe me! My heart was broken, it's still broken! What I did was out of love for you!" Massimo reached for Nonna's hands, but she would have none of it.

"Love for me? Then tell me the reason! *Perche'?* Tell me why you left me without even *Ciao!* All I want to know is... WHY?"

"I can not say. If I do, then you will be in danger again, and so will I."

"So this means nothing! This was your chance to make it right, even with a lie I could believe."

"You think I have not suffered, *Carissima*? Out of misery, I gave up everything!"

Nonna glanced again at his son. "*Ma non tutto,* not everything."

Tony leaned to whisper in Ma's ear. "Did she just insult a Mob boss? How does that work?" But there was more, and she was going to do it in English.

"Shaddap I tell you straight!" She jumped to her feet. "Go to hell!"

She pressed the inside of her thumb against the inside of

her two front teeth, and whipped it out toward Massimo with a gutteral, two-part "Uuuh—UUUH!"

The whole table jumped. She'd renewed the curse.

"Well," Sandro said outside in the car. "I think that went well."

We drove back to the house in silence. It was impossible to say what the fallout from this might be. It was probably best if we didn't share our own versions.

# CHAPTER TWENTY-THREE

## Omens

How much worse could the day go if I stopped by Homicide to see what I could pick up about the Rekler murder, and try and find out where Morgan was? The bigger challenge would be not getting picked up, myself.

I told Sweet Boy to find our way downtown, while I thought things through. Every time I tried to put Nonna's issues aside, they got tangled up in Mob connections, and that just naturally led back to the Precinct and to Frank Longoria. He was more than just a friend to organized crime.

How upset was Vincent Serpa, right now? Who was he blaming, if anyone, for what happened? We'd done everything we'd been asked to do. I got the impression he'd hoped his father would tell the rest of the story, and that he knew what it was.

The BPD parking lot was slammed, and this was a Sunday. Something was up. I got rock star parking close to the building when somebody pulled out just as I arrived. Too easy.

Then the walk down the hall to Homicide went off without a hitch. Nobody gave me funny looks or made cracks about the cemetery thing, or for accidentally marrying a jewel thief. Way too easy.

But I'm a reasonably smart woman, so how could I have let those things take my mind off of what was probably waiting inside... Harper Frasier, yeah, My Harper, the one Vicky had married however briefly. Now that I knew, I felt foolish for nurturing a secret crush on him.

It all came back to me and I practically kicked the door off the hinges. And there he was. Adorable, leaning back in one of those wobbly wooden desk chairs out of the 40's, with his crossed ankles up on the desk. Leather shoulder holster lovin' having to hug that body all day. He was chewing gum, and I didn't care. We never said hello; it was always the same.

"Hey Harper, how's it hangin'?"

"Gettin' no complaints."

"Your boss in? I don't want to see him, I just want to be prepared for the encounter, having left the priest and the holy water in the car."

Harper chuckled. "He's out somewhere. Got a meeting with some bigwig from out of town."

"How big?"

"Very big."

"Law enforcement?"

"Yeah, right." Wink.

Oh my god, Longoria was meeting with Serpa. About what? I had to work very fast.

"Morgan Rekler. Where is she?"

"Dunno."

"Try again." He looked so innocent.

"I always try to help you. I do things any other guy would never do."

"So I've heard." He gave me a quizzical look and I tried another route. "Is she a suspect?"

"Everybody's a suspect, you know that."

"Has she been arrested?"

"Not yet."

That was one good thing. "So then, where is she?"

"She might be a material witness, PJ. She might be somewhere for her own safety."

"Where?"

"Dunno."

"Harper, I have two words for you: Vicky. Ontario."

"Hollleee shit!" He jerked upright and knocked his coffee off the desk. "How'd you find out about that! My fiancée would have a heart attack!"

I choked down the fiancée part and moved on. "So I ask again, where's Morgan?"

"She did it on her own. We did not put her there. Frank doesn't even know this yet. I just found out. Up in the mountains, Shangri Lox." It was a collection of elegant, high-buck "rustic vacation cabins" that its wealthy Jewish creators with a sense of humor had dubbed Shangri Lox.

"Is she alone?"

"Appears to be."

"So who else is on Frank's 'maybe' list of suspects?"

"C'mon PJ, you're killin' me."

Longoria could be coming back any second, and I needed to be gone. As a general rule of thumb, you never wanted to be the person he made first eye contact with. Especially if he'd been eating anything with sugar. Long story. And you never, ever wanted to make eye contact with him if you were *me*.

Nothing. Silence was sucking up precious seconds I didn't have.

"So, Harper, you know how names can be confusing. Should I call her Vicky Frasier now, or are you guys going with Harper Balducci?"

"O-kay, okay, okay, okay. He might be interested in Bridget Simms, Morgan Rekler's mother. The Reklers were headed for divorce, and a mother'd just naturally take her daughter's side. Especially a mother who'd been up for murder before."

"Unfair. It didn't stick." I glided a few feet over to his desk and sat on it for effect, crossing my legs like time was only an illusion, prepared to stay for an answer. It was freezing here; the air conditioner must've been blowing straight down. "Tell me, Harper," I cooed through chattering teeth, "who else?"

"Who else *what*?" The icy voice at the door emphasized the T. "*What*?"

Time had run out.

No one was ever happy to see Frank Longoria. Probably not even his own mother.

*Congratulations, Mrs. Longoria, it's a dear little boy.*

*No it's not, it's Frank.*

"Just killin' time, had to stop in to see a friend of Pop's," I told him. No point making up a more elaborate lie, he wouldn't believe it anyway. He just stood there behind me, would not do the natural thing, would not walk past me toward his office. This forced me to do a complete 180 to face him, like a child.

After which, he said nothing. Didn't even blink. Reptiles do not have a fast blink rate. Finally, he knuckled the brim of his Fedora up enough to take his eyes out of shadow. He liked to look down at a person without bending his neck. It gave the impression he was deciding whether to step on them like a piss ant, or keep on walking. And I understood that the shivers... they had been a warning, another omen.

"You have special friends," he said flatly.

"Thank you. Who would they be?" I asked.

"The question is, what did you do to deserve it?"

"I don't know what you mean." I really didn't.

"I operate by my own rules. Outsiders interfere, here, they do so at their own risk."

Harper sat very still and walked his chair back a couple of feet, out of the way of whatever death rays Longoria might send out.

"I really don't..." Was he talking about Serpa? Had Vincent told New York to lay off?

"Of course you don't, Santini, you never do. Here's what I think," he said, doing a visual sweep of the doorway to his open office, making up his mind whether to peck the flesh off my bones in front of a witness or do it in private, where he could put on a bigger, off-the-record show. He opted to save that for later.

"Here are some facts." All he was missing was a giant blackboard and squeaky chalk, a lab coat, and an auditorium of eager note-takers. "Everywhere you go, somebody dies. Zane Rekler is dead. Murdered. His wife, Morgan, had a motive. She hated him. She had hired a lawyer, several lawyers, to sue him for divorce. This was before – did she tell you? – before she hired you and your boss, Mr. Daly, to investigate her husband, to delve into his financial affairs and to find out what he did, and with whom. Her mother, Bridget Simms, also a suspect. She and Morgan were in the Rekler house on the day of the murder. Neighbors say she left after Morgan did. Time unaccounted for."

He put his hands in his pockets and rocked back on his heels, enjoying it too much.

"And now we come to you. Before her disappearance, Morgan Rekler, who it turns out is your friend, went to yet another group of lawyers and set up a foundation with herself as CEO and you as CFO, in charge of all the cash. It's called "HerSelf". What do you think that means?"

"I have no idea. This is the first I've heard of it!"

"Of course. Regardless, you might have considerable cash to gain in the event she isn't around to control the dollars she automatically would receive from the Pre-Nup she signed with Rekler. There is a clause that gives her even more, if he dies first. And she has directed that most of that will go into the foundation. It's complicated."

I was stunned.

"Oh and another detail, amusing, actually. You seem to be displaying a sudden interest in the art of manipulation and presentation of female sexual wiles. I'm not talking about yourself personally, of course, that really *would* be funny. Rather, your recent acquisition of kinky sexual instruction materials. With whom would you be sharing them? And under what circumstances? Are you becoming an entrepreneur? Setting up a business?" He was walking while he was talking, into his office to pull something off his desk, and out again.

"Huh?"

"Now don't be shy, you know you proudly posed for a security photo with said manual in the bookstore. I believe this is it. *Bad Girl Sex For You*. Not a bad likeness, although your hair could've used some work. This photo is part of your ever-expanding file. Not sure how all this ties in yet. We'll just call it Exhibit A. Exhibit B is some rather interesting store video of your acquisition of sex toys."

Harper moved further away.

"This means," Longoria breathed, "and I relish each and every word, that as you, PJ Santini, have a good deal to gain from Zane Rekler's death, and perhaps from the missing Morgan Rekler, you are a prime suspect in the murder of Zane Rekler. Do not leave town."

# CHAPTER TWENTY-FOUR

## Sinker

N*eed you over here ASAP!*
Pop's text came in just as I was burning rubber barreling out of the Precinct.

Had Morgan set us up, Daly and me? Had she in fact anticipated that somebody, maybe she, would whack Zane, and we would be her pre-murder sympathetic allies? Hiring us because she was timid and "afraid" of her husband... but not too afraid to eliminate him? And what about the money? When I could catch my breath, there'd be a long call to Daly.

But Pop never texted, so this had to be an emergency.

*On the way!* I messaged back and hit the gas, taking Browning to Broadway and cutting over to Casanova to save five minutes.

In Lovejoy, it was complete pandemonium and Tony was at the center of it. A friend had forwarded him a Tweet of a woman's amazing, nude body with my head superimposed on it, doing something with a banana that's illegal in six states and the District of Columbia.

Tony was yelling at his bud for sending it. "Delete! Delete!"

Ma was enraged, and had begun cooking. Nonna was looking for flammable liquids and old newspapers, god knew what for. I told them all not to worry, that it obviously wasn't me because I hate bananas.

Everything stopped.

"Yeah," said Tony, "the banana's the reason."

I was looking for something inexpensive to throw at him, when Pop said, "Lemme see. Nobody showed it to me."

Show such a thing to my father?

"Somebody show it to me! I'm a cop, remember? I've seen worse." Open mouth, insert foot. "Or better. What the hell, show it to me!"

So Tony did.

"Well," said Pop as a blob of melted butter slid off some hot late-afternoon toast, "at least this unspoken message didn't involve any real body parts, like the last one with the finger in your desk drawer. It's clearly an attempt to intimidate you into stopping whatever you're doing, PJ. Dare I ask what you're doing?"

"Could you talk about that later?" Nonna said. "Ama tella you, we got another problem. The things I take pleasure in, I can't do."

"Wait, hold it, I know this one," Pop said. "Tony Soprano again, right?" as he went to answer the ringing house phone.

"Yeah," I said, "definitely. I wish she'd move on."

"The problem is," my brother said, "Something's wrong with Nonna. She's giving me recipes for the restaurant, but they're wacky. Nothing like the way she really cooks, which is her favorite thing in the whole world. Plus, instead of me copying her notes, she insists on dictating. But she's leaving out important stuff; and adding stuff that shouldn't be there. Who would eat *Tiramisu* with slivered garlic instead of almonds on the top? Or *cannoli* stuffed with *ricotta* and sardines with a fennel cinnamon sauce? At this rate, Opening Night will be closing night, *capice?*"

"Nonna, what's wrong?" I put my arm around her and gave her a soothing little squeeze, which was no easy task considering she doesn't clear five feet on a good day, and I'm 6'1" in heels.

"It'sa da curse. It reversed on me. How could dis 'appen. How could this 'appen." Her voice was getting small again.

Pop hung up the phone. I needed to slip him word that whatever he heard from anybody at the Precinct about me and sex, he shouldn't take it seriously. But there was no time for that.

"Well," he said," I got good news, and I got bad news. I'll save you all the anticipation. They're both the same. Vincent Serpa can fix your recipe problem. He's on the way over."

"Now? We've got no food ready!" Ma tied on her apron.

"Take it off. Trust me, it ain't about food. Tony, get your grandmother some *Strega*. Get some for all of us."

Mob boss Vincent Serpa stood on the top step of Dominic and Margie Santini's house and asked permission to enter.

"Mr. and Mrs. Santini, the tragedy that has befallen my father and your mother is a misunderstanding that transcends generations. I respectfully request a few minutes of your mother's time so that I may tell her some things she doesn't know. I will be breaking a promise to my father, which I do not take lightly. But it is for both their sakes that I have made this decision.

"He is on his way back to Sicily. His heart is broken even more than before. He is not well; he has lived many many years. For both their sakes, if it's not too late, I think I can make it better."

He came inside, and my father offered Serpa his personal overstuffed chair. He did it for his mother. The family lined up on the couch, five people on a piece of furniture built for four, with Nonna on the end. Serpa leaned toward her, resting his arms loosely on his thighs like he hung out in the homes of Organized Crime Task Force members every day.

"Thank you for allowing me to talk with you, Mrs. Santini. You are a very gracious and very kind woman. And may I say, also very beautiful. Exactly as my father described you.

"My father was visiting here for several weeks. Just before he was scheduled to return to Sicily, he confided in me. My mother is no longer alive. She never knew any of this, as she and my father met in a part of Sicily far from the place where you and he grew up. He has been carrying this around with him, has been bearing this cross, as they say, for all these decades."

"He wasa so young, we were so young," Nonna said, crossing herself.

"As you know, in Sicily there are so many allegiances and grudges from one village to the next, you need a scorecard to keep up. Feuds are very old. You and my father were never supposed to fall in love, you were never allowed to. But you did.

"Eventually his family and yours agreed. But for my father, there was another problem. A vendetta had existed for generations specifically between his relatives and yours. Most people didn't even remember it.

"But some did. And my poor father was ordered, the afternoon before your marriage, to use the occasion of your wedding to murder your father after the ceremony. Not just murder. A knife to the heart! To symbolize some perceived betrayal committed by your relatives decades before."

Nonna went pale. *"Assasinare di mio padre nel cuore!* Knife to the heart! No no, Massimo never would-a do it!"

"Exactly! He was in agony. He would never do it. He already knew this when you shared your gold *amuleto* with him. When he told you *'per sempre significa per sempre'* he meant it.

"Forever mean-a forever. *Sempre.*" Nonna nodded in agreement and looked at us all, to make sure we understood.

"My father was just a boy. He didn't know what to do or say. If he tried to fight them, he wouldn't win. If he had ignored the order and married you, you and he wouldn't have lived long enough to have children. You would have been in the crosshairs of vengeful men until you died.

"Mrs. Santini, your Massimo saw that in order to save you his only choice was to vanish. To leave by himself, to go to relatives far away without even saying goodbye. One day he would contact his parents. And you... if ever it were safe to do so."

Nonna blinked.

"He tried to keep an eye on you from a distance, to protect you; but then he lost you. You married and moved away. Of course you would. Still, he never gave up the hope of seeing you again, of touching you, of holding you... until this visit to me. In desperation, and believing you were somewhere in Sicily or in mainland Italy, he told me the whole story. And he swore me to secrecy."

"Very hard, *molto difficile* for you, a son," Nonna admitted.

"Yes, very hard. His words haunt my thoughts. I will try to remember them exactly: 'My beloved Giovanna Maria must never know my weakness in not standing up to them. It was not that I didn't love her... it was that I did. Every time I feel this *amuleto* resting on my chest, I can feel her head, her hair, the scent of it. And I am lost and ashamed.' My father said this to me!"

Serpa let it all sink in. Finally, Nonna wanted to know how his half of the *amuleto* wound up here in Buffalo.

"I am sorry to say, my father tore his gold chain from his neck and threw it into the trash in New Jersey, along with his half of the Medusa. He said, 'That is where I belong! In garbage!' Ignoring the obvious, I knew what he meant.

"He had always been a good and faithful husband to my mother, and the best father to me. But to see him like this was terrible. He did not deserve it. So I made inquiries, both in Italy and here in the States. And, it is almost beyond belief that here we are. Here you are."

"But the *amuleto* is here. *Che cosa?* How?"

"It found its way home."

He was right. It might have come via pawn shops, but it had, in fact, come home.

Nonna cried and cried. We all did. The tough broad inside her collapsed as she buried her face in her skirt, and she became again the teenager in love forever, Giovanna Maria with the soft eyes and the head full of dreams. She whispered into the fabric, long caresses of words. Pleas and sighs. And "Massimo, Massimo," over and over, hanging on the esses, burning them into her heart.

"Mrs. Santini, my father still believes that you and your family would be harmed if you and he were back together." He looked very hard at her. *"I'd like to see them try."*

She sniffled.

He opened his hands. "Well, everyone, that's it." He looked relieved and exhausted. He stood, and we all stood.

"My father has gone back to Sicily." He pulled a bulky office envelope out of his suit jacket. "Here is my father's address. Short notice flights are expensive. And a woman should not travel alone. God bless you."

He nodded to Sandro, whom we'd forgotten had been standing in the corner, and they both left in the black SUV that had been idling at the curb.

# CHAPTER TWENTY-FIVE

## In

"Can I borrow your night vision goggles?"

"Excuse me?"

"May I *please* borrow your night vision goggles?" Getting equipment from Daly was tricky, because he always wanted to know why.

"NVG? What for?" He always felt he had to protect me, and I appreciated that, but this operation would be a piece of cake.

"I need to do some nighttime foraging. Indoors. Easy in, easy out."

"We'll talk about it when you get here."

This time I parked to the rear of Iroquois Investigations, which Daly had located deliberately in a forgettable old house, in a block full of them. But to judge it at face value would be a mistake. Everything about it was latest technology, including the security cameras. He could see me, but he liked to stick to procedure and he wanted me to flash my ID. I used to hold up any card as a joke, like my American Express or a promo card from Wegman's groceries. But these new cameras could read everything but my shoe size, so I used the right card because I was in a hurry with no time to play. He wasn't.

"What's the secret word?"

"There's no secret word."

"Oh yes there is. Think about upstairs." And then I knew where he was going with it.

"Beluga." And the door buzzed open.

Daly's upstairs stash of liquid and nutrition for long-haul operations and emergencies included Gatorade for electrolyte replenishment and MRE's (military prepackaged Meals Ready to Eat). But life throws all kinds of situations at you, and my own personal favorite is in the refrigerator marked OTHER, beside the *Dom Perignon*. It's the caviar. I felt one of those emergencies coming on again soon.

"Why night vision? Where?" he asked again, as I extracted my heels from his lush carpet and eyed his outstanding chassis leaning against my desk. So much to lust after. But also so much to respect and admire, that I sometimes found myself marking my territory, waving a Shalimar bottle, for instance, in the private bathroom. Unhealthy for a woman who doesn't want another "relationship". So I pulled my mind back to the point.

"Let me tell you about my day. This morning you brought me Morgan's envelope, which included photos I'm still trying to forget, and a couple of keys that I think I've figured out. Then lunch with Big Vinny Serpa, the New Jersey family boss Sandro works for. It seems his father, Massimo, jilted Nonna back in the Old Country, eons ago. Massimo himself was at lunch. Nonna did not take it well."

"Details!"

"But wait, there's more. At BPD Frankie Longoria tells me I'm a suspect in the murder of Zane Rekler, and he says I've been made the CFO of a foundation Morgan set up."

"True. It's called HerSelf. I located papers on that this afternoon."

"So he wasn't lying. I thought he'd made it up to scare me."

"And the night vision?"

"Hold on, lemme finish painting the picture. This evening, Serpa again. He dropped by Ma and Pa's with the rest of the story. We all cried our eyes out, and he left an envelope with his dad's address in Sicily and enough cash to buy a plane to fly us all over to go see him before it's too late."

Daly lit up. "In other words, you're saying it was a day of betrayed trust, imminent danger, organized crime, and utter chaos. Don't toy with me."

His kind of day.

"So knowing all this, you'd think by now I'd want to run home, sit in a corner, and suck my thumb with a raincoat over my head. But I still want to work, I just need the damn equipment. Whaddaya say?"

"How can I refuse."

"Thanks. I'll be needing a flashlight, the NVG, and a small infrared penlight for reading." I gathered those things and did a quick change into the plain black leggings, sandals and loose black T-shirt that live in my middle desk drawer. Daisy and a spare magazine were tucked into the wide elastic belly band that wrapped around my midriff. I hated it, it was never comfortable; but it had saved my life, so I wore it.

"Will this friendly intervention be in a residence or a business?" he asked while he checked his watch and started locking up.

"Business. Probably after hours. Although the entry could take place at any time."

As soon as I said it I knew he'd have twelve comebacks, but the only one that mattered was the unspoken one, the look that told me I could count on him. That was all I needed.

"Don't do anything I wouldn't do," he smartassed as I swept the goodies into my black leather bag and closed the door behind me.

Kettlebells was open until 8:00 every night, seven days a week. This being an hour before closing on a Sunday, you'd have expected business would wind down. Far from it. Last-minute athletes, both singles and couples with kids, were rushing the doors in an effort to spend a few minutes starting another week with a clean slate.

The valet was off duty. I left the car in shadows as far back in the lot as possible. Sundown wasn't due for about half an hour. The dumpster would have been perfect camouflage, but too risky with end-of-week trash can emptying. On the other hand, on the way out maybe it wouldn't hurt to snag a bag of office papers.

Tagging along with a group of clients, I stuck my head around the corner under that nice front canopy and didn't see anyone familiar inside. A group of women checked in with their key fobs and headed for their Locker Room so I blended in, faking conversation and keeping pace behind them.

For the next forty-five minutes I holed up in a bathroom cubicle, taking a chance nobody would challenge my presence. If it didn't work out I'd just flush and leave, and go to Plan B: the back door and the key, after everybody was gone.

Finally, an employee began the pre-closing check. First, in the men's john. "Yo, anybody here?" No answer, so he moved on to the ladies'. "Anybody home? Hello?" My thought was that if he were to do a visual, the cubicle door was now unlocked and I'd make it look like I was dressing and go on the offensive. *What the hell are you doing in here? Wait till I call management!* But that was unnecessary. He switched off the light, and wasted no time getting to the front of the building. Then all the main fluorescents went dark and he closed up.

Kettlebells used a popular security company, and I knew the drill. I'd have about thirty seconds from the time he armed the system to get to the keypad. The moment he slammed the front door, the goggles were on and I was moving.

His headlights swung across the facade, and I crept up and entered the numbers Morgan had given me. Hopefully it was the code to Kettlebells.

It was.

I hotfooted it to the back, to the first place a guy like Lamar would keep his possessions, legal or otherwise: the Men's Locker Room, took off the goggles and hit the light. The lockers marked STAFF were at the far end, around the corner from the showers. The one that said JACKSON was the last one in the bottom row. The cute little locks most people use to secure their belongings at health clubs telegraph one message: my whole life, in my purse or my wallet, is in here and you can open this toy lock with a paper clip. This lock looked like Fort Knox, big and heavy. And Weiser.

The small key opened it, and of course when I lifted it off I dropped it, but noise wasn't an issue since I was the only one there. The troubling thought surfaced that there might be more to the Morgan-Lamar relationship than she'd said, given that she had the keys and the security code. Daly probably was already there.

When Morgan headed for the mountains and called about her envelope, the cell reception dropped out repeatedly when she was saying something that had "are" in it. It had to have been Lamar. The rest was easy.

His three-foot tall space was crammed with everything but workout gear. A one-gallon red plastic gasoline can, and personal things like a watch and a washcloth. And actual bound ledgers and journals labeled *Clients, Accounting* and *Assets.* The material girl in me reached for Assets first.

*Assets* had nothing to do with things like properties, CD's or bank accounts. It had everything to do with people. Girls and very young women. A double-page for each, with headings including Name, Age, Physical Description, Age @ First, Talents, Turn-Ons, Family.

Family had an asterisk and must have been very important. Under Family there were several options: Involved, Absent, Cooperative, Single Parent, Runaway. And there were photos. Always a pretty headshot tame enough for a yearbook, then more detailed stuff. Very graphic.

Under Talents, there were options for things I'd never even heard of. I almost threw up.

Five of the double-pages had single black diagonal lines drawn across. Probably girls out of the program. Then the flashing red lights. Two of the double-pages were crossed out with big red felt-tip X's .

At that point, I dialed Pop and put him on the speaker.

"I don't know what to make of this, not entirely. The girls with the two red X's are named Linda Coleman and Keisha

Bartle. I'm hoping those names don't mean anything to you and the Ice Pack."

"Unfortunately, they do," Pop said. "Keisha was sixteen years old. A runaway from Greenwood, Mississippi. Coincidentally, she was finally ID'd this morning, or her remains were. She was found in a motel south of town just before Christmas, wrapped in a shower curtain. For reasons I won't go into, it was hard to make an identification."

"I have two other big books, one is people's names and phone numbers, mostly men, and notes about some of the "Talents" they like. The other is financial; I'm looking at nothing smaller than five-figures. Looks like they cross-reference with the clients. But there's a separate section with only initials. FL and a couple of others...I can't make this one out..." I was sitting on the floor with the flashlight, wanting to take photos with my phone but afraid that could screw up the call. "Pop, there are a lot of people, a lot of names. This didn't start just yesterday."

"Where are you?" he asked. "Are you at home?"

"Nope." Didn't really want to get into that.

"Where, then?"

"I'm at a gym, Kettlebells. It's okay. All this is coming with me, so you'll have it. I'm parked out back, leaving right now," I told him as I struggled to my feet and shoved the journals into my bag.

*"Are you alone? Get out NOW!"* Pop yelled, as I hung up.

"No. Stay." Lamar spoke from the doorway, as the lights went on and he pulled a shiny silver 9mm from his back waistband. "I was wondering why the alarm wasn't armed. Then I heard you. Bitches love to talk. Stay with me, my dear. It will be so much fun."

# CHAPTER TWENTY-SIX

## *Danger*

amar jettisoned my phone into the urinal.

"Come with me, and take off that stupid top." Mother of pearl! I wasn't ready for this.

"Tell me something, Lamar. I always liked you, always thought you were pretty cool. A real good advertisement for personal fitness. Why did you get into this line of work?" This might buy some time, but only if he could process bullshit as well as he could dish it out.

"In the eighth grade it was pretty clear that girls liked muscles. Wrestlers, team athletes, it didn't matter how stupid they were, they were heroes and automatically got laid."

"And that got you thinking about a career?"

"It got me thinking about gettin' laid."

"I see." This was going nowhere. Change the environment. "Mind if we move into the other room to continue this discussion? It's just as much fun in there."

"More, even," he said as he stepped aside and motioned with

the gun. "After you." He was so used to winning, he wasn't even considering that this time might be an exception. Especially with a female.

"You're the one who gave Morgan a black eye, aren't you? It wasn't her husband this time, it was you. It was her right eye. You're left-handed."

I wanted to keep him from focusing on me. Wanted to keep moving. It was my impression that he would not choose to shoot, here, at his gym. Too much cleanup, not his style. *Head toward the cover of those metal machines. Get him talking about the Tweet.*

"Was it you who posted that Tweet of my head on somebody else's body, doing that thing with a banana?" I asked as casually as possible, with my blood pressure scraping the ceiling.

"Did you like it? After what you saw at Masters Grand, it was supposed to get you back to minding your own fuckin' business. See, I asked around about you and found out right away you're a detective." Vertical movements with the gun. "Now. Lose the shirt."

"In a minute," I said as we approached the Glute and Thigh machine, the same one a string-thong-wearing Morgan had sat on when she still liked having her picture taken. "How does this thing work?"

When all the humans went home, lone voices were hollow in this cavern of metal and plastic. The paddle fans on the high ceilings were turned off, and the air conditioning was set just low enough to sustain life. Without circulation, the stagnant air gave up the odors it had accumulated all day, perhaps for many days, barely disguised by air freshener and those cleaning wipes they use on the machine seats and handles. We both were starting to sweat. The human body does not respond well to heat. Thought becomes difficult. Behavior becomes more aggressive. Irritability leads to irrationality. I was counting on all of that.

"Lamar, how do you adjust this thing so that you can get a really good inner thigh workout?" That ought to switch the blood supply from the tiny brain in his head to the one south of his zipper.

He gave in, and felt around in the dim light for the pin on the weight stack. It was several weights down, so he leaned in front of me to reach it. Just enough time for me to get my hand on Daisy and take him by surprise.

I got that part, then the front door flew open and another voice tore through the quiet.

"Jackson! You there?"

Apparently it was a surprise to both of us. Lamar jerked up and away.

"You're early. I'm back here! C'mon back!"

"Absolutely not," said Redford Link. He toggled the light switch a few times and nothing happened. Lamar must have disabled it at the breaker box. "Turn on the lights and we'll engage in discussion like civilized people, even if one of us isn't. I want the records. You said you'd give them to me. That's all I require."

"Come back here, I can't hear you!"

"You can hear just fine. You don't need them, with Rekler out of the way. I did it for both of us. He was too powerful. All you have to do is bring them to me, right up here. You get your cut right now, cold hard cash, and it's over, how easy is that. What became of those two girls wasn't your fault. Just part of business. So turn on the lights." He followed that up with the unmistakable metallic sound of a round being racked into the chamber of a pretty big semi-automatic.

By then, I had a solid two-handed grip on Daisy and she thought it'd be a good idea if the two of us got out of that room so the other two could eliminate each other.

"I've got to pee!" I wailed, "and other stuff! I can't hold it! You know how women are!" and lit out for the Men's Locker Room. Nobody followed. After all, who wants to take on a little woman with the runs?

While Lamar dealt with Link, I snagged my bag and the evidence, hit that wall switch to bring on the dark, and made a run for the spot where I calculated the back delivery door would be. The damn deadbolt needed a key to open! So I shoved the bag off to the side and looked for a large, heavy workout machine to station myself behind for cover.

Concealment is nice, it's a place to hide; but I needed cover, something a bullet wouldn't penetrate, although it could always ricochet and get me anyway. I wished I'd thought to put the goggles back on. The going was slow, feeling my way from one machine to another, easing toward the front. Killing the locker room light had made it even darker everywhere else.

Lamar had gone stealth, and there was no telling where he was. Except that he'd been sweating, and I could smell it. It smelled like doom. He was very near, close enough to touch. Could he smell me? The thought was so disturbing, I imagined I must be panting. It was with extreme effort that I forced myself into shallow breathing.

Minutes went by. It was so hot, I thought I was going to pass out. Then, this being a dick-waving contest between arrogant men, one of them made a mistake. Redford Link marched down the center aisle of the fitness club, daring Fate to do anything about it.

It happened that Fate inspired Lamar to take a shot at Link, and the bullet tore through his ear. When he collapsed with a yelp, Lamar took off sideways... and slammed into me.

Our hearts pounded until we got over the shock of it. Then we rolled around virtually blindfolded, gouging and grabbing, making animal sounds with the effort. I was hanging onto Daisy with everything I had, biting his nose and working my free thumb into his eye socket when the bastard bit my boob. Bit my boob!

That was it! I pushed him away with all the violence I could muster and fired off two rounds. Neither connected. *On your feet. Get on your feet! I can't. My ears are ringing from the discharge and I'm dizzy.*

He dropped his gun and easily picked me up, to slam my spine into the side bar of a leg press, sending needles of shock up into my scalp. Then he pulled back to take some fist swipes. For some reason he changed his mind, maybe that wasn't personal enough. We were breathing into each other's faces as his hands closed around my throat.

That was when the martial arts training kicked in. It's all in how you see it. When an opponent has both hands on you, no matter how strong he is you have the advantage of knowing exactly where his hands are. And where his balls are. Instead of wasting time trying to get him off my neck, I stuffed Daisy into my belly band, took him solidly by the shoulders, and unleashed a knee strike that propelled his testicles into his sinuses.

It broke my heart that I couldn't actually see him drop. But the audio was satisfying. I'd had no idea he could hit such high notes.

Link, who knew nothing about me, did know that I was a witness to his confession of homicide, and therefore a complication. He was on his feet, homing in on the sound. He might have made that last move stupidly and it cost him an ear, but he wasn't as impulsive as Lamar. This time would be different.

My first mistake was stumbling over Lamar, whose satisfying moans were giving away our position. Link changed courses and headed directly toward us. We were at about the center of the room, in front of the bank of Ellipticals. My immediate goal was to run behind them, between them and the wall, and get to the entrance. My sandals were making slapping noises, so I took them off and Link had a harder time with that. He paused to listen.

Everything was quiet enough until a scramble of weights that some idiot had left on the floor gouged the skin off my feet. There's something about trauma to the toes that creates a wave of nausea. When it rises in your throat, it's almost as debilitating as the pain itself. And swallowing it in silence is nearly impossible. *Swallow it anyway, damn it, and keep going if you want to live!*

The air conditioner compressor kicked in, and for a moment I thought he was taking advantage of the sound to move around. But then it went off, and there wasn't so much as a shuffle. I listened harder. *Stop concentrating on sound and watch the shadows.*

Being very near the exit was good. Being down low, out of the line of fire, was better. *Shadows along the wall.*

I looked away to scan the environment, to check the whole of the room for movement. I was not so familiar with the place that I knew which dark shapes were supposed to be there, and which weren't. Eventually he'd have to move and cross in front of me. I should look for that, and then I could pick him off. Not cold-blooded, just a fact. It would be him or me.

The space just ahead came into view again, and by the time my pupils adjusted to soft light filtering in from the outside, it was too late. The pale features of the left side of his face, distorted by congealed blood, were suspended above me. The rest of him fell into shadow.

In the next seconds, and they seemed an eternity, his body came into focus. Dimly silhouetted against the window, his feet were a yard apart, standing as inanimate as a practice target. It would have been the perfect shot.

But he raised his muzzle first, I could feel it. One well-placed bullet and his troubles would be over.

"Say your prayers," he mouthed evenly, massaging each syllable, relishing it. A prosecutor's closing argument, sure of a winning verdict before a captive audience. A showman savoring the moment, taking all the time he pleased.

Too much time. Behind him, the door had opened without a sound.

"You first, asshole."

Tango Daly and his .45 . "Drop it or die."

Link, being a lawyer, was skilled at following simple instructions. He opened his hand, and the trigger guard of his gun had just cleared his index finger on the way down to the classy indoor-outdoor carpet, when who should come alive but Lamar Jackson.

Still bent over from the blow to his family jewels, he was limping but making good time, coming up on my right and taking aim at Daly. Or Link. Or me. His sighting was pretty much all over the room.

There were absolutely no options to weigh, no decisions to make. I had to do something fast, before Lamar moved in front of me and I risked shooting Daly. From my position on the floor I raised Daisy with a deep breath and exhaled, peeling off enough rounds to bring Lamar down.

I didn't expect to see Link when I looked back, but it turned out he was better at taking advantage of individuals than of situations. In all the confusion, he'd made no attempt to escape or even to recover the gun at his feet and try to shoot his way out. Daly might have been disappointed about that.

# CHAPTER TWENTY-SEVEN

## Allegiance

"Am I gonna die?" Lamar wheezed, as four wounds bled profusely and we waited for EMS.

"Yes, you little bitch."

If he wanted Mommy-ing, he was talking to the wrong person.

Then, just when the police gave the okay for paramedics to enter and I was feeling a tiny drop of compassion because I'm female, damn it, and I can't help it, he started.

"You too."

"Me too, what?" He was hard to hear, with the gurgling in his throat.

"Place is going up. Should be home with my girlfriend. Link should be with his precious papers, chained to the lockers. He killed Zane anyway, so... fuck it."

*"Oh my god! Everybody out! Hurry! Everybody out! There's a BOMB! Out! Out! Let's GO!"*

Running in the opposite direction when everybody else was heading for the front door was either the stupidest or the bravest thing I'd ever done. But once I got that black leather prize in my hands it became part of me and I blasted off for the entrance in my bloody feet with the bag clutched to my chest. Police cars were leaving skid marks as they relocated onto the street – half the force was there, and more sirens in the distance – with Pop and Daly hanging out the doors of the last vehicle, ready to get me away as soon as I showed up.

Officers had worked fast to block the street, restricting traffic. From our positions behind the cars, we waited for the blast... and waited. EMS had already left with Lamar. Link was getting his ear bandaged in the back of a squad car, where he was trying to figure a way out of this one without any of those handy records to pick through and selectively turn over to lighten his sentence. Daly and Pop were on either side of me. Pop had made the call to Daly as soon as I hung up in the locker room. Which reminded me, I was going to be needing a new phone, as mine was in the urinal. Explosion or not, there are some things I won't do, even for a 5G.

Television news SUV's were beginning to arrive. Renza waved to me from ours, gave me a thumbs-up and blew me a kiss.

Daly stiffened. "Still an amateur." Blowback from the time Daly came across the aftermath of a little situation between Renza and me, involving powdered sugar and my dining room table.

One thing was for sure: this live shot would be mine, if I had to wrestle the mike away from him and stuff his 100% silk pocket scarf up his mouth. But in fact there would be no story tonight at all, and I'd feel really stupid, if there were no explo...."

*Ka-BOOOM!* It wasn't as big as I thought it'd be, but the flames were spectacular. The fire started in the back and spread around the side, to where we'd been gathered when

Lamar started talking. Something was exploding like fireworks all along that edge, shooting green and yellow into the night sky, mixing with the whipping blue lights of the police cars and now the red of the fire equipment.

"Here," Renza said as he shoved a microphone in my face. "And here's the other half." It was a wireless mike, no long cord, so it was in two parts and the transmitter was going to clip onto my waistband, around back.

"Thanks, Johnny."

"So, what're you going to say?"

"I'm thinking. That there's a fire here at Kettlebells, and that officials obviously haven't investigated to determine the cause because it isn't even out yet."

"And the ambulance that just left? What's that, a mirage? That would be the whole reason everybody's here. Police radio, remember? Shots fired?"

"Yeah, right, I get it." Working this out would take time. "The best I can do at this point is report practically nothing because of a little thing called evidence."

"May I ask how you got here so fast?" he wanted to know. I'd wondered how long it would to take him.

"As you can see, I'm wearing workout clothes. I've been looking into what you and I discussed. How's your girlfriend, anyway?"

"Don't change the subject. Who was it? Who got shot? You owe me an answer." He had a point. Renza was the one who'd talked me into pursuing this, and he'd steered me toward Kettlebells in the first place.

"It's the worst possible scenario, Johnny. It'll be a good report someday soon, and you'll regret ever giving it to me, IF I can prove some stuff. It'd be a great report right now if I could use it all, regardless of proof. Let's just say your girlfriend is keeping company with some very bad people."

"I'm no longer one of them. She broke up with me because I told you."

"Now, see, for me that would be like the Super Bowl. I want to care, I know I should care, but I don't care. I'm standing here in my bare feet, all dirty and bloodied up. Help! Heels! I need HEELS! I can't go on the air without HEELS!"

"Thought of that." Renza loped to the van and produced the pair of old, beat up, unwearable *Charles Jourdan* black pumps that I kept in my bottom desk drawer for luck. I was dumbstruck.

"You did this for me? You thought of this?" I'd find out later how he got into my damn office.

"I had no idea what you'd be wearing, but I know you well enough to know that heels make you YOU. What's-his-name over there doesn't know everything," he said, nodding at Daly.

Daly stiffened again.

So thanks to Renza, when I went on the air the facts were the only things that were bare. Even as I was lining up what I was going to report, I fantasized about being able to say it all:

"Another felony crime featuring every taxpayer's favorite duplicitous waste of money, Frank Longoria. You'll have to take my word for it, since I have no way of proving his deep involvement, beyond his initials. The man is head of Homicide, for god's sake." That's what I *wanted* to say. And finish it off with, "The District Attorney will go into Lamar's ledger and compare the dollar amounts beside 'FL' to Detective Longoria's bank deposits. Of course, we all know Frank is too smart to slip up that way." But I couldn't say any of it. This bothered me more than anything else about the complicated story.

At least we got to do the report from a great location right in front of the action, because I was already there when the street was blocked off. Behind me it looked like the Fourth of July at Disneyworld. My story was a little short on facts, but the light show made up for it. Somehow it came to a merciful end, and I signed off:

"We'll have more for you on the Late News. Reporting live from the site of the Kettlebells fire and shooting, I'm PJ Santini."

To be honest, the most dramatic part was when the police tussled with Nonna to keep her off-camera. She'd insisted on riding over with Pop. Every time there was an explosion and more fireworks lit up the smoke, Nonna threw another shower of dried rosemary. Worse, her Harley dude unfortunately had taught her how to whistle with enough authority to stop a bar fight. It was almost as loud as the sirens.

"Hey, hey! Over here!" She blew out a big one, and didn't talk until she had everybody's attention. "PJ Santini, she's a my granda daughter! She needs a gooda man!" Turning to the cop holding her back, "You, for instance!" This guy was a good catch, if ever there was one.

"Pommie!" she yelled over at me. "Pommie! He's not married! I'll get his numbah! Call now, before it's all gone!" She'd segued to the Home Shopping Network. Actually, it wasn't bad.

But I was twice humiliated. Only close family called me Pommie, and only when they'd lost their minds. Now everyone would know me as "Pommie, the girl whose grandmother had to set her up." What if this cop knew Harper Frasier? It would live forever.

Heading toward Pop's car, and just when I thought we could wrap up the evening and I could go home to contemplate it in a hot tub, sipping champagne through a straw, along came trouble. Against the backdrop of police radios delivering the news that Lamar Jackson was DOA, it was the one voice I'd been dreading.

Longoria. Fedora, forked tongue and all. His dark blue un-marked Ford was lurking in a parking lot on the other side of the street. I had no idea how long he'd been there, but I got the impression he hadn't just arrived.

"Get him out." He was leaning in to give an order to the driver of the car that was going to take Redford Link to jail. "Get him out on that side, Sergeant. I want a look at him."

While the officer walked around to pull him out on the street side, Frank and Redford exchanged a glance that could have meant anything. It was friendship, but more, with a low-ering of the lids that suggested an understanding. Then, Frank broke away to join the Sergeant.

"Why isn't this man cuffed?" he demanded to know, catch-ing Link's gaze again, I thought with an imperceptible nod of familiarity, almost shared intrigue.

"EMS just got done treating his ear, Lieutenant. It was almost blown off. I'll do it now." The Sergeant spun him around to cuff him behind his back. But Link kept turning and, using that mo-mentum, initiated a swift series of motions that surprised everybody but Longoria. It was brutal, throwing the Sergeant against the vehicle, smoothly taking his weapon and threatening him with it. Most other attention was on the fire, so this played out only to the small audience of those involved... and to me. The Sergeant put his hands up. The three looked at each other, now what?

When time telescopes and dangerous actions go to slow motion, everything seems to stop, including sound. Yet words weren't necessary to know what was going on there, it was all in the eyes. And I knew it was a setup. Link was going to escape, head back up to Canada, and Frank was giving him the chance.

But before he could make his move, Longoria reached into the jacket of his Eliot Ness suit, drew from the shoulder holster and delivered a change of plan. Now, everything really did stop. Especially for Redford Link.

# CHAPTER TWENTY-EIGHT

## The best laid plans

From the open back seat window of Pop's car, parked far enough away from the fire for safety but within earshot of Longoria, I watched Frank talking with his officers in the aftermath of Redford Link's death. There was no question of his demise after Frank got through with him, and everybody was standing around waiting for the Coroner. They were complimenting him on his terrific reaction time.

"Sure didn't take you long to draw, Lieutenant. Good work. Great shots. The bastard was going to kill all of us."

Frank beamed. "I just got lucky."

He could say *that* again. But if he did say it, humbly looking down at his shoes like a schoolboy, it wouldn't sound right. Self-deprecation just didn't work for Frank.

Then, in the theatrical glow of the colored lights, on this hot summer night thick with death and drama, and with no effort at all, Frank swiveled his head to focus at Pop's car across the pavement and make a laser-sharp connection with me. He held it as his lips parted into a smile. He wanted me to see him tasting victory, to watch helplessly, to appreciate his quickness and cleverness. And power.

He wanted to make the point that my knowing everything was inconsequential. That I should stay awake nights, worrying how he would redouble his efforts to "legally" eliminate me, too, and that in the end he would win. He'd said it before, that it was just a matter of time. Pop picked up on it.

"Sonofabitch!" Pop exploded in the front seat. If Frank thought my father was out of the picture because he was retired, he was wrong. He and his Ice Pack buddies had drawers of organized crime files filled with references to Longoria. They were just waiting for a slip-up. One slip-up. Meantime, Pop didn't want me caught in the middle.

We both wondered at the same time how long Frank had been there tonight, and if he'd seen me run like hell out of Kettlebells with my black bag. It was a beautiful *Coach* duffel for personal travel, so why would that matter to him? Because I was the last one out, and the bag clearly was the reason. It could hold only one thing.

"Do I have to turn it over?" I asked Pop, my touchstone in matters like this.

"You should turn over evidence. But for it to be evidence, there has to be a crime. So far, officially there isn't one. And I don't think he'll be in the mood to take you to court to force it, with his own involvement deeply documented and just waiting for investigators with the juice to get into it. Sonofabitch!"

"Even if you were to give it to him right now," said Daly, whom I didn't realize had walked over to the car, "he'd still know you had the facts in your head, and you'd be as big a danger to him."

"One helluva fire, though." One of the cops was calling Frank's attention back to the group. Look at that." They couldn't take their eyes off of what was left of Kettlebells.

"Oh my god! Sweet Boy! *Sweet Boy!*" He'd been my symbol, had gotten me through rough times, made me smile. When my husband died, I lost his love, his friendship, and the financial support of a successful lawyer. Also all the money in our savings, which he had secretly spent down. He'd left me the SLK and expensive condo payments. Depression distorts your view of life. At the lowest point, I thought that if I absolutely had to, I could always live in the car and shower at Vicky's for awhile. Keep visiting my parents, they'd never know, never worry, never see me as incapable. Sound irrational? Lots of things are. And now, I'd left Sweet Boy parked at the back of Kettlebells. "He's toast!"

"Nah, he's not." Pop's speech was back down in normal range. "Tony and your Nonna rode over with me. Your mother said she couldn't take it, she'd watch the whole thing on TV. I gave Tony your spare set of keys and he rescued your car before all the mayhem started. If you don't count the ride over with my mother."

"Did you happen to see Longoria arrive?"

"He was here when we got here." Pop sat with his elbow propped up on the door, taking it all in, comparing it to crime scenes over his decades as a peace officer.

"Really. Then what about Link? Was his car here?"

"Nope. There was only one other car in the lot besides yours, and that was Lamar's, right out front. And Longoria's was the only one in that other lot. I know exactly what you're thinking."

Theory: Longoria felt so compromised by Lamar's instability, and by the ledgers, that he'd personally given Link a ride over to pick up the books and at the same time kill Lamar, as he had killed Zane Rekler. That would have eliminated the two troublesome humans.

As for troublesome papers, there would be only what Lamar had in the locker. Rekler had gone out of his way to fly under the radar, leaving Lamar and Link to deal with the messy details of business. His interest was purely the final dollar amount.

After the second killing, Link would be allowed to escape and return to Canada, and simply disappear. Longoria then could decide to begin anew with another gym, or let it drop.

"Not a bad plan," Daly admitted, "but it blew up with Link's arrest. When Longoria ordered him out of the squad car, Link still thought he was going to walk. He just had to make it look good, take the Sergeant's gun and back off. Or shoot the Sergeant, it wouldn't matter, Frank's attitude had said as much."

But about that time, Longoria learned Lamar was DOA, and the King of the Double Cross saw an opportunity of his own. He thought quickly, turning against Link and firing multiple shots in "self defense". Link didn't even have time to be surprised.

"Guys like Frank really believe they deserve it all," Pop explained to me through the rearview mirror, "for making the entire operation possible, probably forcing patrol officers to ignore overnight movement inside Kettlebells. Lights, people, pumped up men, eager women, underage girls with big hair doin' things they didn't learn in Math class. This didn't cost him anything, since the officers were rookies who followed orders without asking."

So Frank Longoria walked away the winner again, more powerful than ever. And although I had enough goods on him for an encyclopedia, I couldn't touch him.

Should I be worried about the Mob? I doubted he'd bring these problems to them. He wouldn't want to be thought of as the detective who couldn't handle business. This meant that when danger came to me it would come directly from him, which in my book was worse.

"Tony," Daly said as he opened Pop's car and offered me his hand, "any way you could hang on to PJ's car for the night? We have a lot of paperwork to take care of after all of this, and I thought she could relax for awhile and I'd buy her dinner, then drop her at her place."

"Absolutely!" Tony jumped at the chance, since he hardly ever got to drive anything other than the Cable Company van for work, or the little retro Yamaha *Vino* scooter, a *Vespa* clone, that I kept at the house just for fun. He was going to have to stop signing his nice vehicles over to his girlfriends as a symbol of his good intentions. The shelf life of those relationships after the ink dried was getting shorter and shorter.

"Good idea," Pop said. "Mama, move up, sit next to me. And fasten your seatbelt."

"Sheesh, watsa with that? Ama no little kid! Ama maybe gettin' married again, Sonny!"

"Dear god, is she calling me Sonny to make a point, or do we have to do The Godfather now?" Pop wheeled the big Ford around and headed for Lovejoy. When they slowed to make the turn onto Brooklyn Avenue, she whistled out the window and the car in front of them swerved and jumped the curb.

Ooooof! I threw myself backwards onto the silk sheets, trying to look alluring, but feeling mostly just exhausted.

"You know what I need? Champagne and, don't laugh..."

# CHAPTER TWENTY-NINE

## Flowing

"Champagne and... this will probably gross you out, but it's got 'soothing' written all over it. What our mothers made out of Mandarin oranges and grapes... and bananas and almonds and shredded coconut and mayonnaise. Ambrosia! It's not fancy, but it's comfort food when it's hot."

"I know exactly what you mean. Done." The cork popped on the bubbly. "I even know where to get it. That little Italian place around the corner has it in their To-Go case. I'll order while you relax, Mrs. Peel."

"Okay, Steed." The Avengers! We did look like they would look on some sort of special assignment. All in black. Of course, I was wearing an outfit I'd pulled out of my PI all-purpose Desk Drawer of Mysteries; it had enough stretch to accommodate current dimensions, multiplied by the square root of Godiva truffles that week. In contrast, his wardrobe was designer. Mock turtle made of cotton cashmere and silk knit, sleeves to the bicep, very developed biceps, with close-cut drawstring pants.

We were upstairs at Iroquois Investigations, another world entirely and as far from the events at Kettlebells as a person could get without boarding a plane.

On the way down to his office, he stopped at a closet and casually pulled out a creamy satin padded hanger with a soft ribbon bow. This, from the closet where he stashed his guy stuff: camouflage gear, and web-belted items that packed things I couldn't guess at, along with boots of every description at the bottom.

The hanger held a luxurious, shawl collared, long dressing gown of rich, golden silk. He held it out to me. It flowed like water when it moved.

I stared at it.

He had women's bedroom stuff in here? Why hadn't I noticed that before? I bet he stocked different sizes.

"What's the matter? Don't you like it? It's a surprise."

"Oh, it's a surprise alright. What the hell? Who wore it last time?"

"It's for you. See, look, read the tag." It was not one of those Made in China things with six sets of numbers on a piece of cardboard hanging from a cheap plastic leash. This tag was on thick silk thread with a teeny wax seal closing the loop. It said simply, *Made for PJ*.

It blew me away! I think he was a little embarrassed, I'd never seen him like that. When he left, I cried. See, this is why I don't call having sex with Daly "making love". It has "love" in it. And that leads to relationships, and can't-live-without, and babies and diapers and folding somebody's Jockeys in the laundry room, all of which I'm allergic to.

While he was downstairs, I ran my fingers through my hair to sort of freshen the look, dropped my clothes to the floor, and slipped into the robe. It was so Hollywood glamorous, it even had turned up cuffs. With no super hot lingerie underneath, I had to make the rest of me look fabulous... and time was of the essence.

I flew into the bathroom and stopped cold when I got a good look at myself. My face was flushed, so were my lips. With curly red hair completely out of control, and the golden silk moving even when I wasn't, I looked like a mermaid! Especially with Daly's custom made walls of green sea glass tiles.

This thing of ours, it felt more and more like we were swimming in warm water, just the two of us, with a whole new set of movements that other people weren't part of. It felt so natural.

The food delivery was fast, and Tango was coming up the stairs before I knew it, just in time to keep me from deeper thought about us.

"Check this," he said, holding up a plate on a tray, "they serve Ambrosia on scallop shells! Appropriate to the name, and very Botticelli. Venus also has red hair, although she's not as beautiful." If there'd been a blood pressure cuff in my purse, I would have reached for it.

"You're overdressed," I told him. "I can't hear you with all those clothes on." So he took them off, and turned to face me, reaching behind him for his robe. I was struck again by the power in the man. And the discipline. The time he carved out of his day for working out really paid off.

We settled onto the bed. The room had bright light for work and dim light for monitoring LED equipment. And torchières for moments like this.

"Look, these shells have a top and a bottom. Remind you of anything?"

"Anything?" I said dumbly.

"Yes." He was very serious, as if I should know. "I would call the color 'blush'. Look closely." He opened one and closed it with exaggerated care, opened it and closed it, like Show and Tell. He put his ear to it. "I can hear the ocean!" Then, when he rotated the plate half a turn for closer inspection, it hit me.

"Oh my god! Shame on you!" I shrieked, and reveled in every second of it. "Shame on you!"

He laughed heartily. "You're the one who requested the Ambrosia. You know you love it." There was that word again. As if reading my mind, he said, "Please understand these things would be very difficult for me to say, if it weren't so easy, with you."

I knew what he meant.

"I adore the robe. Thank you. It's very, very beautiful. I can't believe you went out of your way to do this for me." I turned his strong chin to kiss him on the lips. "Plus, you have excellent taste."

"It's all in the reason, PJ. You're the reason."

"Not like your friend – what's his name – with the shelves?"

"He's a genius. He spent some time in a war zone. At the end of a date, he'd tell her to 'take something from the top shelf' or from the second shelf."

I laughed so hard, champagne came out my nose.

"Don't laugh, he was the most popular man there. He specialized in *Bebe* merchandise and good makeup that was being discontinued in the States, nothing they could get there. Everybody won."

Beyond being lovers, we were friends who enjoyed each other's company. Very dangerous. Was I being dragged, kicking and screaming, into an actual relationship? The last time I trusted a man I gave up my career and married him, and everything disintegrated. But then, this time, if I let it happen, it would be Daly. I'd already trusted him with my life, over and over. And he'd saved it again tonight.

There's a lot to be said for the European custom of clicking glasses with someone and never losing eye contact until the drink is sipped. It means something. Granted, in Italy sometimes it means, "I'd watch my back, if I were you." But most of the time it's a special moment. We did that, and we did it again.

When he slipped my robe to just the edge of my shoulders, I appreciated the art of seduction. When he opened the waist tie and let the fabric take its own time falling away, I tried not to think of the circumstances under which he might have perfected it. For a no-nonsense badass like Tango Daly, with the sort of military and off-the-grid background people don't talk about, this sort of behavior, well, it just didn't fit the profile. Which made him all the more appealing.

Just like in the movies, he dribbled champagne into the little well at the base of my neck, and with his index finger he traced a line of it down to my navel, while the rest blazed new trails on my skin. Then he did it again, with his tongue, and I could barely breathe. Was it wrong of me to worry about the silk?

In the next few minutes, I could not believe my good fortune. He was doing so much *so right*, I actually began to feel guilty. So the next time I decided to try my hand at it, and it worked out perfectly!

Afterward, we lay there together and I began thinking out loud.

"I'm going to miss you," I whispered into his cheek.

# CHAPTER THIRTY

## Sea change

"Miss me? Where am I going? Where are you going? The bathroom's only just around the corner."

"Father away than that," I said, tracing the outline of his lips.

"Where?"

"Sicily. We're going to Sicily. Nonna, Sandro, Tony and me. It'll be *The Santinis Take Italy!* Ma's staying home with Pop. It should be noted that this trip will be financed with Vincenzo Serpa Cash."

"Seriously? How's your father with that?"

'What're ya gonna do. It's important to his mother... and to a pretty darn good looking Italian gentleman named Massimo. He's the guy who jilted Nonna at the altar, but with a very good reason, and they've got to make it right. Nobody lives forever. Plus, Tony can pick up more recipes for his restaurant. It'll be with Nonna's blessing. She says it isn't heresy as long as hers get top billing on the menus and a much bigger, bolder font."

After sex, Ambrosia becomes finger food. It's a legal fact. So we were sitting up in bed, picking the grapes and the oranges out of the mayonnaise, and sucking each other's fingers. I know, to a lot of people this would be having too much fun. Which is why I don't ask them. I ask Vicky, who can't ever have too much fun.

"Speaking of weddings, isn't Vicky marrying Sandro soon?"

"You're a mind reader. Very soon. Obviously because she's pregnant and they thought it'd be a nice touch if everybody had the same last name, but she also wants to get married before Nonna visits Massimo."

"It could turn into World War III."

"Exactly. The last thing you want at your wedding is Nonna putting a curse on the very concept of marriage, and forking her fingers at the groomsmen's crotches."

Daly considered not throwing this next volley, but he couldn't resist it. "I hear your buddy Johnny Renza is about to get engaged. But surely you already knew that."

"You're making that up!"

"I am not. As you know, one of your photographers, Billy, does some work for me. He shot a story with what's-her-name. You know, that sexy blonde at your station. Oh yes, Kathy Shula."

"Kathy? You're only pushing my buttons!"

"Kathy told him it will be announced at a newsroom luncheon in the next few weeks. You didn't get the invitation?"

"Impossible! You're playing with me, saying this to make me crazy. He wouldn't do that without telling me. It's just common courtesy."

"Courtesy, like when he was dating that stripper, Honey Summer, who it turned out was the subject of your big story?"

I decided to ignore that, and segue sideways to another subject.

"So, we wrapped up the case that began with Renza's girlfriend's trips to Kettlebells. PS: It appears the bastard was dating both her and Kathy at the same time." I could not turn it off.

"A detail."

"And it began with Morgan hiring you to investigate Zane Rekler. Which turned out to be not such a bad idea. Do we know where Morgan and Bridget are now?"

"Still in the mountains at Shangri Lox. Forensics found evidence at the scene that it absolutely was Redford Link who caused the death of Rekler. And Homicide confirmed it with a servant who was in the kitchen at the time of the argument in Rekler's office. It was so intense, she took off out the back door and was hiding on the grounds when Link followed him onto the terrace. They argued at length, and Reklas sat on his weight bench and went out of his way to act dismissive, like Link wasn't there. Link apparently didn't like being ignored. It went on and on. Eventually, Link slammed the dumbbell into Zane's head a couple of times. She saw the whole thing."

"So that takes me, Morgan and Bridget off Longoria's hit list. But Bridget stayed behind when Morgan left the mansion. Anybody know why?"

"There was some concern about that. But the maid says Bridget was just walking around, whispering and chanting, doing things that reminded her of her childhood in Jamaica, something she called 'planting Karma'."

"Well, it worked. It all came around, nice and neat. Except for Frank, who's still healthy, employed, and untouchable."

"Right. And he won't be giving up on getting you, getting us, out of the way. If not this time, then the next. Which reminds me, where are the ledgers?"

"Nobody knows I have them. They're downstairs by my desk. You and I are the only living people who know they survived the fire. Technically, Pop knows, but only a couple of names. I ask again, would it be a crime to keep them? What case would they be instrumental in investigating, now that Rekler, Link and Lamar Jackson are all dead?"

"If they ask, Mrs. Peel, you will have to relinquish them."

"Fine, Steed, but I won't do it here. I will agree to bring the ledgers to Homicide at an appointed time. Actually, I'd give them only to Harper Frasier, just on general principles. Turning over to Frank evidence against Frank is just not in my DNA."

"Meanwhile, until such time when they might legally be evidence, they can be stored in a safe here at the office. With that explanation attached to them."

He took a deep breath and caressed the nape of my neck, which of course stopped my thought process and gave him an advantage. If you'd given me a million dollars, I could not have predicted what he'd say next.

"Maybe this is the Year of the Wedding. Vicky's next. Then Nonna and her first love, who knows how that might turn out. Food for thought."

And then, no words. He took a long time working his eyes down my real estate, frankly because there's so much of it. But I like to think it was because he was taken with my loveliness. When he reached my navel, he paused. Then with absolute clarity and a wicked grin, he spoke.

"I can hear the ocean..."

...until next time

Turn the page to read the beginning of

# Heels of Fortune!

PJ Santini Series Book 2

# CHAPTER ONE

"I weel suck on your poosy until your ears flaap like those of an elephant!" the deep voice intoned over bump-n-grind background music that bore a striking resemblance to Hockey Night In Canada. The call was coming from my parents' house.

"Nonna, is that you? Hello, Nonna Giovanna? Why are you calling, are you alright?"

"*Aspetta*, wait... no no, not you my love..." she said to the man at her end, then the line went dead. My transplanted Sicilian grandmother was discovering amateur dubbed-in American porn, and the family was trembling at the possibilities.

*That's what you get for answering the phone in church,* I told myself. But it was the other call that really started the trouble. It came so soon, I thought it was Nonna again.

"Not now. I'll call you back," I whispered.

"You have something that doesn't belong to you. I want it."

"Excuse me?" The last time somebody said that to me, it was that bitch Kathy Shula in the parking lot during Senior Prom, trying to repossess the captain of the hockey team. She'd been way overreacting. I was only borrowing him.

"I'll put it in short headlines, so you can understand," he said dryly. "Your husband thought there was only the Polaroid. But there's a cod, a memory cod. You give me the goose, I'll give you the cod."

"Cod. Is this about fish?"

"The carrrd, the memory carrrd!"

"Oh, *carrrd*. Are you from Boston? Who is this? Is this that 1-900-SexTalk number I accidentally dialed last week? You know it's illegal to keep calling me back."

"Remember, you're in the picture, too. If you don't give me the goose, the cod will go to your friends at the Precinct, and I promise you, it will take... you... down. You'll never know what hit you. You have 48 hours. I'll be in touch."

"Wait! What am I, a farmer? I don't have any goose. You have the wrong number."

"No I don't, Ms. Santini, I'm looking right at you."

"Who *are* you?" I demanded, whipping around, craning my neck to search faces. Nobody was looking at me, and nobody was on a cell phone. The guy had hung up. About that time, the church minister walked to center front, stretched out his arms, bent his knees, and made palms-down movements, his eyes fixed on some distant, imaginary chopper he was guiding in for a landing. This being a room full of TV people, it takes more than that to shut us up. So he lifted his arms out to his sides, about shoulder height, and began flapping in slow motion like an Animal Kingdom lake bird. The effect was curious enough that people did start paying attention. And snickering.

We had gathered there to bury our own twisted television colleague, Gerald Sigmund, "Siggy", who'd been running a monster drug and prostitution ring off of his humble newsroom computer. It had gotten him dead. I'd become involved in that case both as a reporter and as a private investigator, but all that was finished now. The only things that were left were spent bullet casings from one end of Buffalo to the other, and glass shards that I was still pulling out of my head from a terrifying episode in a strip joint dressing room.

Droplets of perspiration were running through the expensive *M*A*C* foundation on my upper lip, which did not improve my mood. The stranger on the phone had made me feel really pissy. It's not good to feel pissy at a funeral. So I leaned to my right and decided to take it out on another of his gender.

"Pssst, hey. It's sweltering in here! Was it absolutely necessary for me to wear all this bedroomy crap?" I complained into the man's smooth, tan cheek. I watched the back of his hand slide up and down my arm, and it gave me the shivers, the sort of shivers that make your pupils dilate and drool slide out the corners of your mouth.

"All I suggested was the color," he said without looking. "Two layers of lace and long sleeves was *your* idea. So then, take one of them off."

"Smartass. You know the bottom one is underwear. This was all I had in black. Except for my Catwoman outfit, which would've set the pews on fire."

I didn't think people had to wear black to funerals anymore, but when have I ever said no to Tango Daly, the architect and owner of Iroquois Investigations, and the hottest private detective boss on the planet? Alright, I have, but it's torture every time. So I've developed a hard and fast rule about hard, fast ones like Daly: When I start fantasizing about a possible future, any possible future, I picture myself a year down the road, seven months pregnant, standing in a pink terrycloth robe and fuzzy scuffs in a laundry room, spot-cleaning his Jockeys. I'm allergic to that. But then my little internal voice starts up. *You know if it were Daly, you'd like it. He'd have you propped up on the washer, diddling your spin cycle, and then...* then I tell the bitch to shut up.

My name is PJ Santini. As my full name is pure Italian linguistic pandemonium – Pompeo Jiacobbe Santini, after my grandfather, according to some secret family tradition – I just go by PJ, or sometimes friends call me Janice, or my relatives go with Pommie, which is worse than the original.

The scene of the crime, and love is always a crime, is Buffalo, New York. I'm a decent private detective, and a better television news reporter. Most of the time it's hard to concentrate, because I'm hanging onto life by my fingernails. What with juggling relationships, wacko blood relatives and revolving charge payments, the one thing that calms me is my eight-by-ten-foot walk-in closet. I've got it lined with magnificent high heels. I've arranged them by color, and illuminated them with the biggest, bitchinest crystal chandelier I could afford. It is without a doubt the best-organized part of my entire life. When Nonna sees the shoes, especially the boots with the thin heels, she spits and calls them slut shoes. Then she does one of those dramatic two-way over-the-shoulder glances to see if anybody's watching, and of course no one ever is, and she wants to know what size I wear. Thank god I'm into a 10, twice the size that supports her 4 foot 11-1/2 inch frame.

Speaking of numbers, I just had a birthday and would rather not talk about age. Okay, thirty-something, but that's it.

I've decided age is only a number, and mine is unlisted. When anybody asks, I've got a rehearsed answer that works for me. I just say I think of myself as a well-maintained, midrange convertible that's just out of warranty. Nice paint, a few dings, substantial bucket seats. Buffed up and durable, in Pop's vernacular, but still fun to drive and ready for action.

So there I sat in the crowded church, squished against Daly, wondering about the telephone mystery man who wanted so badly for me to goose him. Daly's thighs felt solid in his expensive Italian slacks, and he smelled faintly of a heady mix of gun oil, mystery and power.

On my other side was Johnny Renza, a fellow journalist and the first boy who ever loved me – literally. His hormones shifted into overdrive in junior high, almost overnight. One day he was childishly walking through the cafeteria at lunch, "blessing" our open cartons of milk with a crucifix that was dropping salt tablets out of a secret compartment underneath; the next day we were making out in the confessional. Wild and charismatic, he was different from the others, more willing to take chances.

In the years that followed, somehow he was always in my life. Then at college, one starlit night in his car, he undid my bra with an impressive flourish and pointed out that we'd known each other for so long, he'd actually watched me grow up. At that moment, I realized in a rare flash of insight that I couldn't honestly say the same thing about him. He hadn't grown up at all, and I didn't think he ever would.

So I started looking around for more mature candidates. Before long, I snagged myself Lou Bonmarito, a law school grad. Much to my family's delight, he asked me to marry him and I said okay. Ma and Pop cheerfully cleaned out their Pommie's Wedding Savings Account, which had been accruing interest ten years longer than they'd thought it would, and the family threw a big Sicilian blowout with dreams of grandchildren dancing in their heads.

Forty-eight hours later, Lou was dead. A damn heart attack on our honeymoon. You can't make this shit up.

These days, the men in my life are the ones I work with. Including Renza, who also went to journalism school and is a fellow reporter at my Buffalo television station. His beat is crime. My beat is anything they'll give me. My work is every bit as good as his, and more than once my intelligence, intuition, and certain other body parts have outpaced him in getting a story. But that same female equipment also gets me the dopey assignments, while he enjoys the challenging ones. He does it by bluffing.

Just look at him. Renza is the only person I know who could get away with wearing a white linen suit to a funeral that isn't in the Bahamas. He has everybody snowed. Women fall all over him because of his dark, wavy hair and big, moony Italian eyes; men wish they could manufacture the same cocky attitude and trademark look. Renza. Johnny Renza.

"Check it out," he whispered to me, angling his head toward the gaggle of plainclothes, gum-chewing cops collected in the side doorway of the church. "They even brought long lenses."

"Why are they here?" I asked him.

"They're Longoria's eyes and ears. You'll notice the bastard's not here himself, but he wants to make sure we're all behaving."

Frank Longoria is another guy I grew up with, a juvenile delinquent-turned-Senior Homicide Detective. I know where his skeletons are buried, and he knows I know it. But when I reported on our infamous recent shoot-out during the final phase of the Gerald Sigmund case, I couldn't tell it all. I'd had to leave out Frank's connection to The Mob, because I couldn't exactly prove it.

He wanted to keep it that way. His boys would be busy taking notes today, for purposes of intimidation and possible retribution. Not just with me, but with anybody on the guest list, and the guest list looked like a Who's Who of *Criminal Minds*.

Eventually we adjourned to our cars and made the drive to the Olde Town Cemetery. It occurred to me that this was the one time we knew beyond a shadow of a doubt, after slippery Siggy's Central American drug operation finally blew up, exactly where the elusive creep really was. Every car in the funeral procession had its air conditioning jacked up in the stifling summer heat as we snaked along Remembrance Way, which ironically had been named for veterans of foreign wars, not foreign scores. After a couple of turns, we parked and made the uncomfortable walk to the grave.

The hot ground by the casket sucked up my black patent leather stilettos like soft cement. Sweat trailed down the center of my back, as I made an unsteady effort to shift my weight without leaning on either Daly or Renza. Both would consider that foreplay.

An hour later, we'd wrapped it up and everybody was grateful to be headed out, when a guy shouted over from three tombstones away.

"Hey! Do I look crazy to you?" I wouldn't say his eyes were spinning around like Marty Feldman's, but it was hard to tell which one was looking at me.

"That would depend on your definition of crazy," I told him.

"They're trying to make me believe I'm insane, but I'm as solid as you are."

As me? That would be a problem. "How can you tell?" I shouted back. "Everybody who's crazy swears they're not."

He dragged his shovel over and leaned an elbow on it, while he wiped sweat out of his eyes with the back of his other hand.

"Well, I know what I know. I dug my ass off last night getting a plot ready for today, and today the damn thing isn't here. It's gone."

"Are you telling me somebody stole a hole? Are you a gravedigger?"

"Cemetery maintenance specialist. Willy Short's the name. I use a machine for most of it, then I finish it off myself. Last night I dug it, today it's solid ground with three inches of grass growing on it. Wanna see?"

"Uh, no." By now Renza had bailed – the chickenshit – and Daly had backed off to enjoy the show. Turns out Willy Short had been digging alone in the moonlight, and his only companion was *Evan Williams Kentucky Straight*, not what you'd call a reliable witness. Still, when he came-to in his own bed this morning, his overalls had new dirt on them, just as you'd expect from someone who'd been digging.

"This isn't the first time. Say, you're on TV, aren't you? Will you explain to my boss it's not my fault? Now there's no place to bury Lola."

Everything in me said *Get out while you can!* But I could not help myself. "Okay, Mr. Short, I'll bite. Who's Lola?"

"That's cute, 'I'll bite'. Lola can't bite anymore. She's a Schnoodle. Or she was."

"What's a Schnoodle, some religious sect?"

"It's a sort of a hypoallergenic cross between a Schnauzer and a Poodle. Over there, across that row of hydrangeas, in the pet cemetery."

That was it. Purely out of habit, I lobbed an Iroquois Investigations business card at him – I sure didn't want him calling me at the station – and took a fisted swipe at Tango, who was standing there grinning with his arms crossed. As usual, he was faster and caught my wrist before I could do any real damage; also as usual, I couldn't wait to try it again later. There was something about the way the breeze caught his shirt, the way the black silk settled over his toned chest… it made my head fizzy.

"Want a ride?" he said seductively as he strode easily beside me. His ride was a fancy BMW 700 series command post. A black stealthmobile that housed every piece of covert operations equipment that wasn't already in his two-story, locked-down private office. I wasn't positive how he got the name Tango; but I knew he'd been US Army Special Forces, had done unspecified covert work afterward, and had enough martial arts expertise to slice you like bacon. I was glad I was his friend. An enemy would have a bad day.

"Very funny," I told him over my shoulder. He knew my ride was still the Toad, a pathetic, worn, green automobile the insurance company had generously loaned me when my pet, mint-condition silver Mercedes SLK, named Sweet Boy, had been ripped off right under my nose. But I'd never given up hope: around every corner, in every parking lot, I expected to see Sweet Boy again, and I wasn't going to settle for buying anything else. The Toad accepted that he was only a temp and took me downtown anyway, to my condo in Erie Towers on Lakefront Boulevard.

This former marital love nest was now pricey and refinanced, but I did have that glamorous minimum wage television job, along with spotty private eye assignments. Besides, the mortgage company and I have a special, environmentally-conscious understanding about late payments: I don't burn unnecessary fuel driving around town to find more work, and they save trees by simply emailing me the routine foreclosure notices.

I used the condominium Electropass to open the underground garage gate, and swiped it again to take the elevator to the sixth floor. I really appreciated living in a secure building. I needed all the distance I could put between myself and obsessed newscast viewers who were convinced we had a meaningful relationship. Like the IRS Tax Examiner who, according to the IRS's own Internal Investigations department, had actually set up an "altar" to me in his apartment.

"But don't worry about it," they said, "it's just a little altar."

"Oh really? Then why did you come to me? Why are you telling me this? Why did you go into his house?" No answer. But it didn't stop there. The jackass shot out one of my tires on the expressway and then, when I pulled over to phone for help, he pulled in behind me and asked, all innocent and helpful, if there was anything he could do. What he didn't know was that my friends at CID, Criminal Investigations at the police department, pulled the file they already had on him and easily ID'd him for me. It put him back on their radar, and on my ever-growing shit list. And that was just the latest stalker.

I exited the elevator onto my floor, and tried again to fall in love with the purple-flecked orange industrial carpet the Condominium Association had insisted on putting in. It looked like fresh chopped prunes in orange juice, and so much like somebody had just thrown it up, that you'd constantly run the toe of your shoe over it to see if it smeared. The configuration of the carpeted landing was square; each floor had four pretty big corner apartments. The area was deserted and the air was stuffy, as I turned the key in my lock. It felt so good to step into the security of my living room, and breathe in the rush of fresh air off Lake Erie. It would have felt a lot better, if I'd actually been the one to have left the sliding glass balcony doors open.

Someone was here! I swung inside, hugged the foyer wall and pulled out Daisy, my trusty Sig-Sauer P230. She lives in a black nylon holster strapped to my thigh, with a little pink ribbon bow sewn on the snap.

I began a room-by-room search. Living room. Dining room. Kitchen. All clear. I could see most of the bedroom reflected in the mirrors of its sliding closet doors, so I wheeled in and brought the muzzle of the gun in line with the center of the bathroom. Nothing. Maybe I really did forget to close the balcony doors. Still, the texture of the place had changed. Things seemed, well, off. Someone had been here, I was sure . Just as I'd felt it the day I came home from my husband's funeral. Both times, a person would have known exactly where I was, and that there was no way I'd be home unexpectedly.

But what could anyone possibly want? That first time, I'd been too shocked to think about it. I'd become a widow just two days after I'd become a wife. I admit relationships can have a shelf life when you really get into them, but this one hadn't even been opened all the way.

I holstered Daisy and kicked off my heels, then flopped down on the bed and wiggled out of everything else. The nice thing about living on the sixth floor in a condo that faces Lake Erie is that you can walk around in the buff with the drapes open anytime you want. And this time I really wanted. I detoured to the kitchen for a glass of Chianti, and took my time ambling toward the balcony, digging my toes into the soft, champagne-colored carpet. The feeling of the air on my body reminded me how unfair it was that men could go topless in public, and women couldn't. I took another slow sip, roughing up my long, frizzy red hair, thinking I had a decent shot at looking hot if I had to. At that exact moment, a savage the size of a Kodiak bear in a dark ski mask came charging off the balcony and body checked me.

"Wha…! Uuuff……!" The blow knocked the breath right out of me and slammed me into the drywall. I could feel the coolness of the paint against my back as I slid down to the floor. An electric wave swept through my limbs, along with the chilling revelation that I was completely helpless, and at someone else's mercy. The last thing I remember before everything went white was the sound of his voice as he made tracks for the door.

"Nice tits, sweetheart."

Made in the USA
Coppell, TX
13 March 2021